Hurry up and fetch all of
the Good Dogs adventures!

Good Dogs on a Bad Day

Good Dogs with Bad Haircuts

GOOD DOGS
ON A BAD DAY

Rachel Wenitsky & David Sidorov
illustrated by Tor Freeman

putnam

G. P. PUTNAM'S SONS

G. P. PUTNAM'S SONS

An imprint of Penguin Random House LLC, New York

Visit us online at penguinrandomhouse.com.

Library of Congress Cataloging-in-Publication Data
Names: Sidorov, David, author. | Wenitsky, Rachel, author. | Freeman, Tor, illustrator.
Title: Good dogs on a bad day / David Sidorov and Rachel Wenitsky; illustrated by Tor Freeman.
Description: New York: G. P. Putnam's Sons, 2021. | Series: [Good dogs; 1] | Summary: "When a
group of well-behaved dogs realize how much fun a little mischief can be, mayhem ensues"
—Provided by publisher.
Identifiers: LCCN 2019050345 (print) | LCCN 2019050346 (ebook) |
ISBN 9780593108444 | ISBN 9780593108451 (ebook)
Subjects: CYAC: Dogs—Fiction. | Adventure and adventurers—Fiction. | Behavior—Fiction.
Classification: LCC PZ7.1.S526 Goo 2021 (print) | LCC PZ7.1.S526 (ebook) | DDC [Fic]—dc23
LC record available at https://lccn.loc.gov/2019050345
LC ebook record available at https://lccn.loc.gov/2019050346

Printed in Canada
ISBN 9780593108444

1   3   5   7   9   10   8   6   4   2

Design by Eileen Savage and Suki Boynton
Text set in Chaparral Pro, Archer, and Johnston ITC Pro

For Molly, Freddie, Whiskey, and Rosie
—R.W. and D.S.

For dear Auntie Kate and her Gus!
Love from Tor xx

CHAPTER 1

"WAKE UP, ENRIQUE! Rise and shine!" Hugo said to his human boy, just like he did every morning. "Time for another fun and busy day!"

Hugo knew that to Enrique, his words just sounded like some excited whines and panting, but he was confident he was getting his point across. Hugo dropped a granola bar on Enrique's face (for Enrique's breakfast) and also brought a tennis ball (for Hugo's fetch).

I wonder if Enrique will want to play before or after he eats, thought Hugo. *Or, whoa, maybe before* and *after? And during?* He wagged his fluffy golden tail and nudged Enrique's arm with his head. It had been a while since Enrique had wanted to play *at all* in the morning, but maybe today was the day!

"Ugh! Come back in ten minutes!" Enrique said, rolling over in his bed and gently pushing Hugo away.

But Hugo knew that ten more minutes could make

Enrique late for camp. Hugo liked to think of himself as not just the family dog, but also the family's assistant and schedule keeper.

So he hopped onto the bed and licked Enrique's face even more playfully. *Enrique can't resist waking up and playing with me now,* he thought.

"Ugh, golden retrievers are the worst alarm clocks ever!" Enrique exclaimed.

Weird, thought Hugo. *I feel like I'm the* best *alarm clock ever. Most alarm clocks can't even drool!*

At least it was working. Enrique was now awake and unwrapping the granola bar. Hugo tried nudging the tennis ball toward the bed again.

"Not now, Hugo," Enrique mumbled groggily. He got up and kicked the ball away, sending it rolling under his dresser.

Great, Hugo thought. *Now I'm gonna have to stare at the bottom of this dresser for an hour.* But first, he had more work to do. He made his way to the next stop on his morning route, the kitchen. Surely the rest of the family would be happy to see him, and maybe someone else would want to play.

But Hugo quickly realized how wrong he was. The kitchen that morning was pure madness. Mom and Dad

were running around wildly in their nice work clothes, barking at the kids and at each other. Zoe had accidentally spilled milk all over the table and was trying to push it back into the glass. Sofia was frantically running around looking for her backpack. Mom was shouting up the stairs to make sure Enrique was awake, while Dad was finishing packing everyone's lunches.

Hugo took a deep breath and quickly got to work making everyone's lives easier.

First he grabbed Sofia's soccer cleats from the hall closet. Sofia was ten in people years, and very good at soccer, even though Hugo still didn't understand how humans could run without falling over, since they had only two legs.

Hugo padded back into the kitchen with the cleats hanging from his mouth just as Mom was asking Sofia, "Don't you have soccer today?" Perfect timing, as always!

"Thanks, Hugo," said Sofia, grabbing the cleats and shoving them into her backpack.

All the kids—Sofia, Zoe, and Enrique—had started running out to wait for the camp bus when Hugo caught something out of the corner of his eye. It was Zoe's lunch, still sitting on the counter! Zoe was the youngest, only five years old, and was always forgetting things. Hugo whined and barked until Mom noticed the lunch bag and called out to Zoe. She ran back in, and Mom put it in her backpack. There, that was better!

"Thanks, Mom!" Zoe yelled, running back out the door.

"Thank Hugo!" Mom replied. "Oh, Hugo, I don't know what we'd do without you!"

Just doing my job, ma'am, thought Hugo.

"He'd be better if he was still a little puppy, though," said Zoe. "Puppies are so fun!"

Hugo looked down at his front paws sadly. When he

was a puppy, everybody had fawned over him. Then he grew up, and everyone got busy. Should he have stayed a puppy? Was that even possible? He'd have to look into it. Mom quickly covered his ears with her hands, but he could still hear what she said.

"You don't mean that, Zoe," she said. "You need to grow out of this puppy phase."

"I'll never grow out of it! I love puppies," said Zoe. "They're so tiny and cute and new! I want a puppy for my birthday. Don't forget. If I don't get a puppy, my birthday will be *ruined*!"

Zoe could be a bit dramatic. But as he watched her put on her backpack, he was struck with a memory. Back when he was a puppy, that backpack had belonged to Sofia. He used to crawl inside of it before she left for pre-school, and he was so small that he could fit his whole body in there with his little head poking out, barking happily. The whole family used to laugh and laugh, and talk about how funny it would be if Sofia took Hugo to school. Enrique would run around singing, "Backpack dog! Backpack dog! Hugo is a backpack dog!"

He loved making them laugh, but it had been a while since he had done anything that silly. If he tried crawling into Zoe's backpack now, there was no way he would fit, not to mention it would make her late for the bus. Hugo missed the feeling that he was making his people happy just by being himself. Maybe his family *hadn't* become too busy. Maybe he'd become less *fun*. He tried to shake off this thought, lift his tail, and return to his normal, helpful self.

"Well, you'd better think of some other presents you might want," Mom told Zoe. "Or it's going to be a pretty disappointing birthday."

Hugo gave Zoe a big lick on the cheek. *No hard feelings,* he thought. *Kids will be kids.*

Zoe sulked out the door right as the bus was arriving, and all three kids climbed on.

Suddenly the house was very quiet, but it still wasn't calm. Mom and Dad were buzzing around, grabbing all their papers for work and putting them into various folders and briefcases. Hugo didn't know what they did all day, but he guessed it had something to do with paper. Maybe they ate the paper? If so, they were very lucky.

Hugo grabbed another tennis ball and pushed it toward Mom, but she waved him away.

"Not now, Hugo! I'm sorry."

That's okay, thought Hugo. *I still have lots to do to keep busy. I'll just go get ready for my morning walk.* So he went back to the hall closet, picked up his leash in his mouth, and sat by the door.

Finally Mom noticed him.

"Oh no," she said, looking at Hugo and then at her watch. "I have a nine o'clock meeting; I can't walk Hugo."

Dad looked at his watch and frowned. Humans were

always looking at their watches and frowning, Hugo noticed.

"I'm teaching a class at nine fifteen," said Dad.

"Well, he'll just have to go to Good Dogs, then."

"More doggy day care? We spent two hundred and fifty dollars there last month! For that price, Hugo should be learning how to read and write."

Hugo knew this was a joke, but he was a bit disappointed that Dad didn't realize he *could* read. It was just that whenever he tried to read out loud, everyone told him to stop barking.

Hugo followed the conversation back and forth.

"What else can we do? He needs to get exercise."

"I thought Enrique agreed he would start walking him in the mornings. That kid *begged* us for a dog. And now—"

"You know the kids love having a dog, but—" Mom looked down at her watch again. "Oh shoot," she groaned. "I really have to go."

She grabbed Hugo's leash, and they headed out the door, down the tree-lined street dotted with charming little houses. One of those houses, around the corner, was Good Dogs.

Hugo liked going there. The owner, Erin, was really nice and always gave good pats and scratches, but he couldn't get something Mom had said out of his head: *The kids love having a dog, BUT . . .*

But what? Hugo had always thought he was an essential part of the household. The fuzzy, drooly glue that held it all together. Was he wrong?

"WHO'S A GOOD dog?"

Startled awake, Lulu opened her eyes to find the wide brown eyes and eager smile of her owner, Jasmine, two inches from her face.

"Who's a good dog?" Jasmine asked again.

It was early, and Lulu was still waking up, but she knew the answer right away. *Easy,* she thought. *It's me.* She wagged her tail.

"Who's a *very* good dog?"

These questions are all so easy, Lulu scoffed to herself. *Me again.*

"Who's the cutest, most beautiful, perfect, sweetest doggy in the whole wide world?"

Okay, whoa, a curveball, thought Lulu. *This is a tough one. Sweetest* and *cutest? Hmm.* She thought for a moment. *All right, got it,* she concluded. *It's me!!!*

"You're my good dog! Yes, you are! Yes, you are!"

Yes, I am! I was right! I was right! thought Lulu.

Jasmine scratched Lulu all over, and Lulu gave a big hanging-tongue smile.

"All right, Lulu, time to get up!"

Lulu stretched her legs and rolled over onto her side. She wished she could stay in her cozy bed—which was made of memory foam, covered in pink satin sheets, and had a velvet canopy—for just a few more minutes. Lulu realized her bed must have been unusually fancy for a dog, because every time one of Jasmine's friends came over, they'd say, "Lulu's bed is nicer than mine!"

Lulu 🖤 9

But you had to work hard to deserve such elegance. That was why Lulu always listened to Jasmine when she said, "Get up!"

So, Lulu got up that morning the way she always did: perfectly. She did everything perfectly. She walked perfectly, she ate perfectly, and she wagged her tail perfectly (keeping it at a respectable seventy-degree angle at all times). Lulu knew that getting up was just the first in a long line of perfect things she would do today. After all, there was a reason more than half the captions on the @LulusPerfectLife Instagram read simply, "Perfect."

Did being this good ever get a little boring? Lulu didn't have time for thoughts like that. She was too busy doing her best downward dog (or, as she liked to think of it, a "downward ME!"), then leaping into Jasmine's open arms and licking her owner's face.

Ah, the face, Lulu thought to herself. *A little salty, but really the most delicious part of the person.*

"Today is a big day, Lu!" Jasmine said.

Lulu didn't need to be reminded. If everything went as planned, today would be the day Lulu and Jasmine hit five thousand followers on Instagram. Lulu didn't know much math, but she knew that five thousand was a very big number. Possibly the biggest number in the world, judging by how excited Jasmine was to reach it. Hitting that number would surely place her among the

♥, Lulu

ranks of the greatest celebri-dogs on Instagram, like MollieTheCollie, Sir Maximus Bark, and Lil' Stinky.

But most important, today Lulu and Jasmine were going to get a pedicure together to celebrate! A pedicure for Jasmine, a pet-icure for Lulu. The perfect day.

"Let's get to work," Jasmine said excitedly as she pushed open double French doors to reveal Lulu's closet. It was filled with every outfit, costume, and accessory a dog could ever want. Everything was bejeweled, bedazzled, and be-eautiful.

My closet would make the queen jealous, Lulu always thought. And of course by *queen*, she meant Beyoncé.

"Okay, Lu, what do you want to be today?" asked Jasmine, holding up several outfits. "A ballet dancer at a construction site? An astronaut on vacation? A pickle at a rodeo?"

They had been through many outfits already, and didn't want to repeat, so they were starting to get creative. Just yesterday Lulu had dressed up as a lobster in a tuxedo (and it had gotten 2,032 likes!).

Jasmine held up the pickle costume invitingly, but today Lulu had something a little more *glamorous* in mind. After all, her fans at the salon were going to want to take a lot of selfies with her, so she needed to look her absolute best. She walked over to her "diva" outfit—a rhinestone-studded vest with a matching skirt, pillbox hat, and sparkly high-heeled shoes—and pawed at it gently.

Jasmine nodded thoughtfully, her hand on her chin. "Of course," she whispered. "Your fashion sense is, as always, flawless."

Once Lulu was in her fabulous outfit, she walked over to the dog-length mirror to take a look. At first she barked—there was *another* Yorkshire terrier staring back at her! WHO WAS THIS IMPOSTOR IN HER HOME?! Even worse, she was wearing the exact same outfit! A true fashion faux paw!

Then she realized it was just her reflection. What a relief! *Mirrors,* thought Lulu. *One day I'll figure you out.*

Ding! Lulu heard a timer go off, which could mean only one thing:

"Time for breakfast, girl!" Jasmine exclaimed.

Lulu followed Jasmine to the kitchen and delicately climbed up the tower of pink velvet pillows to take her place at the table. Today's breakfast, for both girls, was a goat cheese tartine with poached egg. Lulu's favorite! Jasmine adjusted their plates to get the best lighting and snapped a few Instagram photos from different angles. Lulu knew that breakfast was a very important meal, and that photography was a very important part of breakfast.

When Jasmine was finished, Lulu dug into her meal—daintily, of course, taking small, enthusiastic bites.

"Lulu, I had the most bizarre dream last night," Jasmine said. As Jasmine chatted, Lulu remembered a dream of her own. She was completely naked *in public* at the dog park, and everyone was staring! She didn't even have a bow, or a tiara, or anything! Thankfully, it had just been a dream.

"And that's when I noticed it was *me* the whole time!" Jasmine finished, and Lulu realized she had zoned out and missed the whole dream. She would make sure to listen more intently next time. She knew that a good dog listens, even when her human is being a bore.

"Time to snap some pics," said Jasmine, and Lulu struck a pose. They got some runway photos of Lulu strutting her stuff, some "Just Chillin'" photos, and, as always, some silly face photos for fun. Jasmine showed them to Lulu, and Lulu barked to pick her favorite: the one where she was wearing big, heart-shaped sunglasses and pretending to read a celebrity gossip magazine.

"Right again. This one is so good," Jasmine agreed as she selected a filter. "What should the caption be...? Ah! I know. 'Woke up like this. Hashtag LulusPerfectLife,'" Jasmine said as she typed.

I didn't *wake up like this, though,* Lulu thought. *You put me in this outfit!* But she didn't protest. It was a good caption, even if it wasn't exactly #true.

Jasmine read Lulu some of the best comments from the day before.

" 'OMG, what an adorable face!' " Jasmine read.

"More please," Lulu said with her eyes as she nuzzled into Jasmine's lap. Hearing from her fans made her feel special and inspired her to be the best dog she could be.

"DogGuy24 says, 'What a floofy poof!' He says that on every picture of you, actually. He's kind of obsessed."

Well, I am a floofy poof, Lulu thought. *DogGuy24 isn't wrong.*

" 'I'd love to meet Lulu someday! She seems like such a good dog!' "

Wow, another smart person. One thing Lulu loved about the internet was how everyone was always so polite, thoughtful, and correct.

"Ooh! Before I forget, I should go get your special T-R-E-A-T!"

Lulu wasn't positive, but she had a feeling those letters spelled *snack!* So she started wagging her tail accordingly. Jasmine came back with a treat Lulu had never seen before: a dry-looking, greenish bar with the unmistakable smell of the ocean.

"It's an organic dehydrated seaweed bar! The company sent it free, just for you!"

Well, it doesn't smell good, thought Lulu, *but maybe it tastes good.* So she took a bite.

YUCK! It did not taste good, either.

"I know it's a little gross, babe, but we have to take one picture with it, for sponcon."

♥. *Lulu*

Lulu knew that *sponcon* was short for sponsored content. That was when companies paid Jasmine to post pictures of Lulu using their products. Sometimes the products were fun toys and yummy treats, but sometimes, like now, they were gross and weirdly slimy.

"You know," said Jasmine. "This treat hasn't even been released yet. You might be the first dog to try it."

Even though it tasted like dry, salty garbage, Lulu felt proud knowing that *she* was the first dog to try this particular dry, salty garbage. So, with Jasmine's help, she pretended it looked interesting for the sake of the photo. This part of the job wasn't always fun— pretending to like something she didn't—but it was all part of being a Famous Personality with an Instagram Following.

"Oh my gosh," exclaimed Jasmine. "We've been having so much fun getting you glammed up that I haven't even gotten dressed."

Jasmine unpinned her hair so that it fell around her shoulders in soft curls, and then Lulu watched as she scrambled around, looking for the perfect outfit. Jasmine's closet was much smaller than Lulu's, but she usually had a much harder time deciding what to wear.

She probably also wants to look glamorous and selfie-ready for the nail salon, thought Lulu. *Good thinking, Jasmine!*

"I have a *huge* audition today," Jasmine said.

Lulu pricked her ears curiously. *That's odd,* she thought. *Auditions usually take a few hours. I wonder if she'll do it before or after our pedicure.*

Jasmine was an actress who went on lots of auditions, but she rarely described them as "huge." Now she was busy explaining why this part was the "role of a lifetime" while she shimmied into a black dress, boots, and a fuzzy cardigan.

"My agent said a lot of girls are going in for the part, but I know I'd be *perfect*. It's a woman who tragically dies and then comes back as a ghost! Watch this!"

Jasmine suddenly stood very still in the middle of the room. Her eyes went blank. She gripped her stomach with her hands, and started to *act*:

"How could you do this? How could you, Sandra?! I thought we were friends! Sandra. SANDRAAAAA!!!" She lifted her hand to her forehead, fell dramatically onto the bed, and lay there motionless, letting her tongue fall out of her mouth.

Then Jasmine sat up cheerfully and turned to Lulu. "So? What did you think? Be honest."

But Lulu just whined, her mind still on the pedicure and how they'd probably be late if they didn't leave soon.

"Hey! I worked really hard on that! I thought I pretty much nailed it."

Lulu turned her head away, unimpressed.

Why does Jasmine care so much about this audition? Lulu wondered. *Auditions can't be nearly as fun as glamorous photo shoots and pedicures with me.* Lulu couldn't sassily toss her hair, but if she could have, she would have.

"Whatever," said Jasmine. "I have a really good feeling about this audition. But hey, it means we have to reschedule our pedicures this afternoon."

Oh no. Lulu whined again and buried her face in her paws. She had really been looking forward to their pedicure date.

"I know, I'm sorry. But you'll be doing something just as fun!"

That's when Lulu realized that Jasmine was grabbing her leash and her special travel bag, which could only mean one thing . . .

"Okay, girl, let's get you over to Good Dogs!"

Lulu's tail stiffened and dropped. She huffed. Good Dogs was the doggy day care that Jasmine's neighbor Erin ran. It wasn't so bad, but it was full of *dogs.* And Lulu didn't really think of herself as a "dog." She was more of a tiny fancy person with a tail and fur and, only once, fleas.

"Oh, come on," said Jasmine. "It'll be fine!"

Yeah, maybe if she were any other dog! But she was not—she was @LulusPerfectLife!

GRASS, SQUIRREL, TREE, *grass, bird!* Those were just a few of the thoughts racing through King's head as he ran through the park.

Grass, bush, bee, another dog, squirrel! More grass!

Wow, for a one-year-old puppy, I sure am good at noticing things, he thought as he tried to keep up with his owner, Erin, and his sister, Cleo, a German shepherd mix. King wasn't sure exactly what breed he was—Erin said he was part border collie—but he knew that Cleo's legs were twice as long as his.

So many dogs in this park, and from the smell of it, they all have butts! King mused, before getting distracted by several more smells.

What's that smell? A spot where another dog peed? Wow! The world has so much to offer! Should I go smell it? he asked himself. *Should I pee there too? No, I should keep running.* But then it hit him: a smell so exciting he forgot about the pee spot.

It was the smell of HOT DOGS. There must have been a cart nearby. King had never eaten a hot dog before (they weren't included in the strict diet Erin fed them), but now the beautiful scent of grilled meat wafted toward him and made him stop in his tracks. Where was it coming from? *It must be just over—*

"King! You can't just stop moving. We're running!" It was Cleo, who had turned around, urging King to keep up the pace.

"Sorry, I just smelled some hot dogs! Do you smell those??" King panted breathlessly.

"Those aren't for us!"

"But they have 'dogs' right there in the name . . ."

"Come on, King," Cleo said. "If you want to be a good dog in the agility contests, you need to learn to FOCUS! Stop being such an *amateur.*"

King knew he was acting a little scattered, but those hot dogs just smelled so amazing! He whined, and Erin tugged on his leash.

"Let's go, King! Keep up the pace!" Erin said.

King started running again, trying to forget the salty, fatty smell of the hot dogs. He did want to be a good dog in the agility contests. He wanted to be better than last time.

"I will learn to focus," King called to Cleo, who was several strides ahead of him. "I am a serious dog! You'll see!"

Cleo and Erin were both older, taller, and faster than King. He had to run really fast to keep up with their pace. *Boy,* he thought, *I'm going to collapse as soon as I get home!*

KING WAS RIGHT: He collapsed as soon as he got home. His legs were tired (from running), his tail was tired (from wagging), and his nose was tired (from smelling pee and hot dogs). He and Cleo rested under the kitchen table while Erin worked the blender.

King was starting to learn what the blender sound meant: smoothies for Erin and her boyfriend, Jin, and homemade dog food creations for King and Cleo.

By the time the blender was done whirring, King was digging into his mix of hard-boiled eggs, peas, oatmeal, and cottage cheese. It was NOT his favorite, but Erin said these breakfasts would help "maximize his potential," and she seemed to think that was really important! It tasted VERY different from the puppy food he'd eaten at the shelter (which was dry and crunchy) and also very different from how he imagined a hot dog might taste (probably hot and delicious), but if it would make him big and strong and help him do better at his next agility competition, he wanted to eat as much of it as possible.

At the last contest, King had come in second to last, which Cleo said was not okay. In his defense, there was SO much grass to smell! He had just gotten a little distracted. Erin had told him it was fine; he'd do better next time. But King knew Erin hadn't taken him home from the shelter to have a distracted, grass-sniffing, second-to-last dog. He wanted to make her proud!

Just as he was finishing up his breakfast, King noticed something out of the corner of his eye. It was Jin, coming downstairs with a box covered in ribbons and colorful paper. And he was walking right toward Erin!

"What is that?" wondered King. Something about the look on Jin's face told him that it was something special. "It looks like some kind of TREAT! Is it a treat?!" King wagged his tail eagerly.

"Calm down, buddy, and don't get any funny ideas," Cleo responded. "It's a gift for Erin. Today's her birthday."

It was as if a million peanut butter bacon biscuits exploded in King's head. He couldn't believe it!

"OH MY DOG, OH MY DOG!!! HER BIRTHDAY?!? WHY DIDN'T ANYONE TELL ME? I LOVE BIRTHDAYS!!! IS THAT HER PRESENT? WOW WOW WOW! ERIN LOVES COLORFUL BOXES! JIN IS SO THOUGHTFUL!"

Cleo rolled her eyes. "No. The present is what's inside the box."

"So, you're telling me she gets a box, a ribbon, AND whatever's inside the box?! Wow! Best birthday ever! I wonder which one she's gonna eat first!"

"You have so much to learn, King."

"CAN I GIVE HER A PRESENT?! WOULD SHE LIKE A BIG BONE, DO YOU THINK?! I WOULD!!!"

King jumped all over the couch, wagging his tail maniacally. Then he darted around the room.

"Whoa there, King. If you want to give her a present, you can start by not freaking out so much. Calm down."

"How do I do that?" asked King, his body moving uncontrollably every which way. When he tried to stop his tail from wagging, the rest of his body wiggled wildly. And when he tried to stop the rest of his body from moving, his tail went berserk.

"I don't know," replied Cleo, calm as ever. "When I get too jazzed, I just ask myself, 'What would a cat do?'"

But King was no cat. When Erin opened her gift, and

King caught a glimpse of what was inside—a beautiful, colorful scarf!—he started yelping.

"*I LOVE IT!*" cried King, his tail speed ticking up to roughly three hundred wags per minute. "*THAT IS THE BEST SCARF! HAPPY BIRTHDAY! WOWOWOWOW!*"

King whined with excitement, jumping up on Erin's legs.

"I love it!" Erin beamed. "Thank you so much, babe! I'm going to put it on right now. It's too cute to wait!" Erin gave Jin a hug, then bent down to pet King in his favorite place: UNDER THE CHIN. And that's when it happened.

"Whoa, did you seriously just do that?" Cleo asked, disappointed.

King looked down and noticed that he'd had a little accident on the tile floor. Whoopsie. He'd just gotten so excited! Who hasn't gotten a little too excited and peed on their owner's floor?

Erin and Jin both started laughing. "That's okay, King! You're still a good boy," Erin said while Jin cleaned up the mess.

But Cleo gave him a stern look. "Rein it in."

After the commotion died down, Jin left for work and, one by one, the other dogs started arriving. Erin was the owner and sole employee of Good Dogs, a doggy day care run out of her house. King and Cleo loved getting to hang out with so many other dogs every day—and they definitely took pride in being the teacher's actual pets.

The first dog to arrive was Petunia, a six-month-old pit bull with a *lot* of energy. She was small but super strong and loved to play.

"Hello, Petunia."

"Hello, King."

"Wrestle?"

"You got it."

And so it began: another day, another playful wrestle with Petunia. They went at it in the grass of Erin's front yard, and by the time they were tired out, several other dogs had arrived, including King's good friends Lulu and Hugo.

King walked over to say hi. They were listening to Patches tell one of his long, complicated stories. Patches was a wise old sheepdog who had really seen it all.

"And then he threw me the stick, and I went and got it and brought it back to him. And then he threw the stick again, and I went and got it again. And then you won't believe what happened next. He threw the—"

"Hi, everybody!" King exclaimed. He had trouble focusing on most of Patches's stories.

King told Lulu and Hugo he was excited to see them as they all sniffed one another's butts hello.

"I didn't know you were coming today!"

"Neither did we," said Lulu, sounding a little disappointed.

"Our people were just really busy today," said Hugo. "But it's okay. We'll have fun."

Lulu huffed.

"Okay, everybody, time to go!" Erin called out. On cue, all the dogs lined up perfectly in front of her.

"Sit," she commanded, and they did, without hesitation. All six of them were very good dogs, and they knew it.

Erin leashed everybody up, and they started walking to King's favorite place: the dog run at the park! Despite their excitement, all the good dogs walked patiently and perfectly. Nobody pulled too hard on the leash or wandered away from the sidewalk.

At the dog run, Erin let everybody off their leashes. King knew what that meant.

Time for me to run around in a circle twenty times in a row!

When he was done with that, he joined Lulu and Hugo in the shade of an oak tree. They were talking to Nuts the squirrel.

"I know I buried them yesterday. I just don't remember where." Nuts was nervously pacing.

"Looking for your nuts again?" King chimed in.

"Yes! Have you seen them? Please, I'm desperate."

"They're under the elm tree," Lulu said nonchalantly. "They're *always* under the elm tree."

King knew Lulu was right. Every day, the squirrel would forget where he'd put his nuts the night before. It's why they all called him Nuts, even though his real name was Squirrel P. Nutsington.

"I don't know. Why would I bury them under the elm tree?" Nuts asked.

"Because you always do," said Hugo.

"I don't think so, but I'll check. Just to humor you."

Nuts scurried over to the elm tree while Lulu,

Hugo, and King walked back toward the other dogs. In the background they heard Nuts exclaim, "Wow! You were right!"

King watched as a labradoodle entered the park with its person. The labradoodle walked over to a bichon frise and said hello.

"Sorry I'm late. I was eating my owner's homework," King overheard the labradoodle say.

The labradoodle and bichon frise both laughed, and then the labradoodle turned his head as his owner took out . . . a BALL.

WOW! thought King as he inched closer. Just moments ago, there was no ball. Now there's a ball!

SQUEAK! The labradoodle's owner squeezed the toy.

And not just any ball, thought King. A squeaky ball!

"Bouncy balls are great," King said, turning to Hugo. "And I love squishy ones. But squeaky balls are the best kind! They make a noise when you chew them! How cool is that?"

Hugo gave him a look. "What about toys that are bouncy, squishy, and squeaky?"

"Are there such things?" asked King.

"You're such a puppy," said Lulu. "There are so many different types of toys, you wouldn't even believe. I know, because I've been sent so many to try."

King watched as the labradoodle and his owner

played fetch with the squeaky ball. *It would be so easy to go over there and take it.* But then he remembered what Erin always said . . .

"Good dogs don't steal balls," said Cleo, right on cue. She always seemed to know when he was thinking of doing something a little bit bad.

"I know," said King. "I wasn't going to! I was just getting closer to listen to that sweet, sweet squeak."

Just then, the gate clanked open again, and a teenaged boy King had never seen before walked in, dragging a French bulldog behind him. The dog had black fur, a white patch on his chest, and a rebellious look in his eye. The teenager was busy staring at his phone, not paying attention as he unclipped the leash and set the dog free, so he barely noticed when . . .

The bulldog went totally wild!

He jumped up onto benches, climbed onto laps, and knocked people over! He started licking the faces of humans he didn't even know! The good dogs stared in shock as this aggressive stranger ran around barking at everyone and everything.

His owner didn't seem to notice or care; he was still staring at his phone.

Meanwhile, the French bulldog chased the labradoodle around the dog run. The labradoodle got scared (King could understand why) and dropped the squeaky ball. And what happened next shocked all the good dogs in the park: The strange new dog STOLE the squeaky ball, ran away to the far corner of the dog run, and started to rip into it with his teeth!

"Who is that?" Lulu asked.

Hugo looked unimpressed. "I've never seen him before."

The labradoodle's owner looked on helplessly, trying to console his pet. Erin stood up, looking upset, and got the teenager's attention, but he just sort of shrugged and kept sitting there. So she took matters into her own hands and marched over to the French bulldog herself.

Erin reached for what was left of the squeaky ball.

"Drop it," she demanded. King had heard that voice before, and knew she meant business.

The bulldog ignored her. Erin wasn't used to being ignored by dogs. All her dogs were good! She tried again, but louder. "Drop it!"

The bulldog growled at her. Lulu gasped. Nobody growled at Erin like that.

"Well, he is a *French* bulldog," offered Petunia. "Maybe he only speaks French?"

But King could tell the bulldog understood English and was being naughty on purpose. Looking Erin right in the eye, he tore apart the ball, then chewed and spit out all the shreds and scraps!

Erin was speechless. The good dogs were barkless.

The French bulldog let out a proud, stubborn bark, and King could have sworn he heard a squeak in there somewhere.

Before Erin could decide what to do next, the French bulldog suddenly lunged at her and grabbed the end of her brand-new scarf in his teeth. He pulled on it, and it became untied. That's when King started to feel upset.

"Don't you dare!" yelled King. "Not her birthday scarf!"

"Who does this dog think he is?" called Cleo.

"No! Give that back!" cried out Erin, but the French bulldog held on to the scarf and ran away toward a picnic table.

"Stop!" King shouted, lunging after the bad dog.

"Yeah!" said Hugo, following after him. "You can't treat Erin like that!"

Lulu cleared her throat and then yelled, "BAD DOG! VERY BAD DOG!" Lulu had learned all about bad dogs from the Bad Dogs of Instagram hashtag. As she'd told King and Hugo, she devoured their adventures like T-R-E-A-T-S, but *she* certainly was not about that kind of life.

Lulu's "stern" voice was just as soft and high-pitched as her normal one, but King had never heard her this angry. Now all three of them were running after the French bulldog, but Erin restrained them.

"Shush," she said. "Good dogs don't attack other dogs."

Well, good dogs don't steal your birthday scarf, either, thought King.

Erin turned to the bulldog's owner again. "Young man! Your dog just took my—"

But before she could get the teenager's help, the French bulldog climbed on top of the picnic table, scarf in mouth, and launched himself over the chain-link fence of the dog run. Just like that, he was gone!

King couldn't believe his eyes. He turned to Lulu and Hugo, and they all stared at one another in shock for a moment before running over to the fence to see what would happen next. Where was the bulldog going? What was he going to do with the scarf? Would his owner even *try* to stop him? But most important . . .

Who *was* this dog?

CHAPTER 2

LULU WATCHED AS the teenager ran to the edge of the fence, too late to catch his naughty Frenchie, who was well past the gates of the dog run by now.

He half-heartedly called after his dog, "Napoleon! Napoleon!"

But it was a lost cause, and the teenager seemed to know it. It was clear who was in charge, and it wasn't this kid.

"That dog has my scarf!" Erin yelled as she quickly leashed up Lulu and her other five dogs and led them out of the run and into the park. They found Napoleon furiously digging a hole near the fountain at the center of the park. *Ugh,* thought Lulu. She would never ruin her perfect nails by digging in the ground. Unless it was for a photo shoot where she was dressed as a bulldozer.

Lulu cringed at the thought of how much trouble Napoleon would probably get in if he kept up this behavior.

He's just digging an even deeper hole for himself, she thought as he dug an even deeper hole for himself. Then Napoleon stopped digging for a moment, only to start up again right beside it!

"What could he possibly need two holes for?" Hugo wondered aloud. "It's almost like he's just digging for *fun!*"

"Come back, boy," cried Erin as she ran toward him. But it was too late.

Napoleon had jumped into the fountain and started splashing. The scarf was nowhere in sight.

"He looks like he's enjoying himself," said a small voice behind her. It was King, who was staring at Napoleon with a mix of disgust and admiration.

"Don't be such a puppy," snapped Lulu. But deep down, she agreed with King . . . just a little. Napoleon didn't seem the least bit sorry. He looked like he was having the time of his life.

The teenager ran around the fountain in circles, calling after Napoleon, but this only seemed to make matters worse. Napoleon was darting all over the fountain now, getting everyone wet and making a scene. Lulu felt a small splash hit her ear. *How dare somebody mess up my perfect ear?* she thought. But then she realized it did feel a *little* refreshing on this hot day.

Finally, the teenager grabbed Napoleon and attempted to put on his leash. But Napoleon was still soaking wet and slid right out of his owner's grasp, making a beeline for the hot dog stand.

"Oh, *there's* the hot dog stand," said King.

Oh no, thought Lulu, *this isn't going to end well.* And she was right, as always. As if in slow motion, Napoleon barreled at full force into the hot dog stand, which toppled over and sent hot dogs flying through the air onto the ground. *Under other circumstances,* thought Lulu, *hot dogs gently raining down from the sky would actually be kind of beautiful. Instagrammable, even!* "Hot dogs and a hot dog," the caption could read. But at this particular moment, it was just chaos. As the floppy beef plopped down softly onto the grass, every dog in the park tried to drag their owners over to the free lawn meat.

Lulu would never eat a hot dog off the *ground*. But then again, they did smell really good. A small part of her wondered how it would feel to act like a *dog* for once. To race over there and devour some meat without a care in the world. Of course, she knew that wasn't something one of the "Top 40 Most Perfectly Refined Dogs of Instagram" would do, but she was curious . . . Plus, she couldn't help but think that a dirty hot dog was probably still better than the dehydrated seaweed that was now sitting awkwardly in her tummy.

King whined as he stared longingly at the hot-dog dog pile, and before she knew it, Lulu heard herself whining too. Then Erin snapped, "Don't even think about it! Any of you! Are you kidding me?"

Lulu was mortified. What was she thinking? Whining at a pile of gross, grassy hot dogs? With no gourmet whole-grain mustard in sight? She snapped herself out of it and sat up straight.

The teenager finally gained control of Napoleon, who had just finished off his fifth hot dog. As he dragged the dog away, Erin tied up her own dogs' leashes to a bench and marched over to the teen, calling, "Hey! Young man! What's your name?"

"Finn," the teen replied, but then Lulu couldn't hear anything else, because he was immediately swarmed by a bunch of grown-ups.

"Wow," said King, turning toward his friends. "That looked really fun."

"What do you think they're talking about?" Lulu asked.

"Punishment, probably," Hugo answered. "He was being *bad*. When Zoe stole one of Sofia's birthday cupcakes, Mom took away her screen time. Maybe they should take away the bulldog's screen time—aaand I see now how that doesn't really apply here."

"You know, back in my day, we didn't have squeaky balls to chew on. We had to chew on *rocks*," started Patches.

"What are you talking about? You're twelve. You definitely had squeaky balls back then," replied Cleo.

"Really? Then why did I chew on so many rocks?" asked Patches. "Let me tell you—"

But Lulu interrupted him before he could launch into another old tale from his past. "Maybe they're congratulating him?"

"But they all look so serious," said Hugo.

"At least they're paying a lot of attention to him," Lulu responded. "In fact, maybe we should all just jump into the fountain," she added sarcastically.

"Maybe we *should*," said King, with a gleam in his eye.

"No way," replied Hugo. "That's the wrong way to get attention. Look how angry Erin is! It's better to ask for it the right way: by lying on your back with your legs in the air and crying until a human rubs your belly. That way—"

Hugo stopped talking as Erin huffed back to the group, red-faced and furious.

"Some people," she exclaimed, grabbing their leashes and dragging them off. It seemed as though dog park time was being cut short for the day. "Reckless dog owners!"

"See?" said King to the other dogs. "She's mad at the boy, not at Napoleon."

"Oh please," snapped Cleo. "Don't be such a—"

But Cleo never got to finish that thought, because at that moment, King suddenly pulled hard on his leash, forcing Erin to drop it. Now free, King ran away, his leash bouncing behind him like a kite, and took a running leap into the fountain.

Erin stared at King in complete shock. She tried to speak but could only get out the words "What the . . . ?" Petunia yelped with delight, while the other dogs couldn't believe their eyes.

Lulu watched King dog-paddling (or, as she liked to call it, "ME-paddling!") around in circles. She would never jump into a fountain and ruin a perfectly luxurious blowout . . . but she had to admit, King looked like he was having the *most* fun.

What's wrong with me today? Lulu thought. She usually knew better than to think like some kind of . . . dog! But she couldn't help but stare at King, playing in the water. And on a hot day like this? It looked kind of, sort of, in its own way . . . #perfect.

Some children nearby noticed King playing in the water, and they came closer to watch. They were laughing and cheering.

"Must feel a little nice to make those kids laugh . . . ," Hugo said quietly to Lulu. Then he shook his head and frowned. "But no. No. It's the wrong way to get attention!"

♥. *Lulu*

Erin ran after King, grabbed him out of the fountain, and scolded him. "King! What were you thinking?! You're a *good dog*."

King whined and shifted his paw.

"Let me see." Erin lifted King's paw and took a look. "Uh-oh. You have a cut on your paw pad. Now you can't go to the agility contest tomorrow! We need to go to the vet tonight and have them take a look at this."

King's tail drooped down between his legs as he rejoined the group. He looked sad and embarrassed.

"Guys, I think I may have been kind of . . . bad," he said.

"Ya *think*?!" Cleo scoffed. "And on Erin's birthday, no less. I can't believe you would misbehave like that! She trained you better than this. You should be ashamed. Ashamed!"

"This is worse than when ol' Frankie Two-Bones ate Erin's left shoe back in '09," said Patches.

"Oh, come on," said Hugo. "He feels bad enough already. Plus, that cut doesn't even look that bad. Nothing a few licks won't fix." Hugo reached out with his own tongue and started licking King's injured paw.

"There. All better?" Hugo asked.

But it wasn't all better. Lulu could tell King felt bad, and not just because of the scratch. He whimpered a bit as they started the walk back to Good Dogs.

"You know," continued Patches. "This all reminds me that I never finished my story about the stick. What happened was that he threw it to me, and then I . . ."

As Patches droned on and on, Lulu took one last look over her shoulder at the fountain. She knew that Napoleon was being *bad*, no matter how much fun he seemed to be having. And that she and her friends were good dogs, and that good dogs had to act a certain way.

But . . .

Had she spent so much of her life acting like a tiny fancy person with a tail that she had missed out on what it felt like to act like a dog?

The whole rest of the day, Lulu couldn't get that look of pure joy in King's eye as he splashed around in the fountain out of her head. Something that fun couldn't be *all* bad.

Right?

CHAPTER 3

HUGO WAS TERRIFIED. He cowered in the farthest corner of his backyard, all the way behind the swing set, past the old, rusty mini-trampoline that no one used anymore, at the very edge of the wooden fence. He had one goal: to be as far away from the house as dogly possible. Hugo loved the house, of course, and especially loved what was inside—his toys, his food, his special blanket— but he couldn't go in. Not today. Not now. Not when the *thing* was in there.

He shuddered. Just the thought of the *thing* sent a chill down his spine.

It was a very hot day, and Hugo panted to keep cool, but still, there was no way he would enter his air-conditioned home while the *thing* was roaming from room to room, wreaking havoc and making that wretched sound. No room was safe. And nothing, not even the sound of his favorite squeaky plastic doughnut, could make Hugo go in there while the *thing* was doing its . . . *thing*.

His eyes narrowed as he stared at the house from a safe distance.

It had been a full day since they'd seen Napoleon at the dog park, and once again, Hugo's family had been too busy to take him for a walk. In fact, they had barely noticed him this morning, between shouting about who had forgotten to do their chores, and tearing apart the hall closet searching for a lost soccer shin guard. Hugo had remembered it was under the couch, but other than one quick pat on the head, nobody had even thanked him. And the thought of walking him seemingly hadn't even crossed anyone's mind.

Then, before everybody left, Dad had done the unthinkable: set the *thing* loose inside the house.

Hugo sighed heavily and lay down in the grass.

What a terrible day, he thought.

He wouldn't have had to deal with this if he'd just gone to Good Dogs, like usual. But Good Dogs was closed for the day while Erin took Cleo to compete in the agility contest.

Hugo rolled onto his side and let his tongue flop out of his mouth. He considered playing with some of the old toys in the yard, but he'd chewed through most of them a long time ago, and plus, they were always more fun with a person on the other end.

I guess I'll just roll from one side to the other, and occasionally stand and bark, until everyone comes home, he thought. *Yes, that seems like a good plan.*

Just then he heard a tiny sound in the distance, like a little high-pitched trumpet. His ears perked up. The tiny trumpet was saying, "Hugo!" It was Lulu! She was shouting at him from the other side of their shared fence.

Hugo loved living next door to Lulu. It was nice having someone to bark with on days like this.

"Come to the gate!" Lulu shouted.

Hugo went the long way over to the gate, staying far away from the house. "Lulu! What are *you* doing home?" he asked. When Lulu wasn't at Good Dogs, she was usually with her owner, Jasmine. She went everywhere with Jasmine. She was very lucky to be exactly purse-sized, Hugo thought.

"It's simply awful," Lulu said, dramatically covering her face with her paw. "Jasmine got a *callback*."

"I get called back all the time!" said Hugo. "I go outside and then I get called back in because it's time to eat!"

"Not that kind of callback," Lulu explained. "Jasmine auditioned for an acting job, and a *callback* means they liked her so much, they want to see her again!"

"Oh! So it's like when I go and get the ball, and I do

such a good job that I get *called back* and they throw it again. I see. That sounds like a good thing!"

"Oh, Hugo, don't be so naive!" Lulu lamented. "If she gets the part, it means she's never going to have time for me *ever again*!"

Hugo thought Lulu was being a bit overly dramatic, but then he remembered that his family had very little time for *him* these days. Maybe Lulu was right to be nervous.

"This morning, Jasmine even forgot to put me in an outfit," she continued, getting more upset. "Now I look like . . . a DOG! I can hardly bear it."

Hugo blinked, confused. "Lulu," he replied carefully. "Don't take this wrong way, but you *are* a dog."

Lulu ignored him and kept talking, this time more to herself. "I just always thought that I was Jasmine's BFF. Her Best Furry Friend. But I guess acting comes first." She stared off into the distance, and a look of despair flashed across her carefully groomed face. But with one big sigh, the expression vanished, and for the moment, Lulu was back to her regular self.

"Anyway," she said, looking down at her manicured nails. "What are you doing outside? It's so hot, it's practically boiling! Doesn't your house have air-conditioning?"

Hugo explained that he couldn't be inside because

the *thing* was in there, causing chaos. He tried to keep his cool. He could easily get riled up talking about the *thing*, and he didn't want his friend to see just how upset he was.

But Lulu was absolutely *furious* on his behalf! She let out a very displeased bark. "How dare they!" she huffed. "When they knew you'd be home all day, no less. Sometimes owners have no sense. They're treating us like we're *dogs*."

"But we are dogs," Hugo reminded her again.

"But we're supposed to be family!" Lulu squeaked.

"It's okay," Hugo insisted. "Luckily, I left a lot of fur on the rug—"

"Shedding season."

"Tell me about it. So anyway, the *thing* was distracted enough that I was able to escape through the doggy door."

"Hmm?" Lulu replied. "Oh, you mean the ME door."

"Sure," Hugo said. "Anyways, I'll just stay out here in the corner of the yard all day. Maybe at some point I'll move over to the other corner. It's fine."

"No!" shouted Lulu. "I will *not* stand for this! It is a *grave injustice*, which I'm pretty sure means it's not fair! If Jasmine ever got a *thing*, I would do just about anything to make her get rid of it. I would pee right in her favorite purse, Hashtag NoRegrets."

Hugo was beginning to feel upset. He didn't like talking about the *thing*. "Lulu," he pleaded with her. "Please. I really don't want to talk about this anymore."

"Okay," she agreed. "I'm sorry, Hugo. But listen . . ." Lulu got closer to Hugo and started talking very quietly, forcing Hugo to lean his head right up to the fence and listen very carefully. "I have a plan to get us outta here," she said slyly. "I know how to get the gates open so we can escape and go for a walk."

Hugo whined. This did not sound like a good plan. It sounded dangerous. "But Lulu," he exclaimed. "We're good dogs!"

"And what good has that ever done us?! Our owners don't even appreciate us. Mine left me outside, completely nude. And yours let that *thing* take over the house. *Your* house!"

Lulu was staring at him with an intensity he'd never seen in her before. And there was a look on her face he couldn't place. It almost looked . . . naughty. There was a moment of silence between them, but it didn't last—suddenly, they heard the *thing* whirring and howling from the living room, startling them both. Hugo buried his face in his paws with a scared whimper.

"Look," said Lulu, calming down slightly. "We'll just walk around until the *thing* is done."

"It's never done," said Hugo, and he felt the fur on his back stand up. "It never gets tired, or stops being hungry. That's what makes it so terrifying!"

Lulu looked Hugo dead in the eyes. "All the more reason to get out of here," she said. "Just for a bit."

Hugo groaned. He had a bad feeling. But then he nodded. Getting away from the *thing* might make him feel better. Plus, he was trying to be more fun. Maybe getting out of his comfort zone would help him loosen up a bit. "Okay. But just for a little while."

Lulu wagged her tail and pushed an old broomstick under the fence. "Just pick it up with your mouth and use it to push that latch on the gate," she instructed.

Hugo was very coordinated—he could even turn a doorknob with his mouth—so he was easily able to maneuver the broom and get the latch open. He nosed open his gate, walked over to Lulu's gate, and slid the broomstick back under the fence to her.

Lulu opened her gate and strolled regally out of her

yard, her head and tail held high, then started trotting across Hugo's front yard and down the street, in the direction of Erin's house. Hugo ran to catch up with her.

"Where are you going?" he asked. "Good Dogs is closed today."

"We're going to check in on King, obvi!" she replied, tossing her head back. "After the stunt he pulled yesterday, I bet he's home alone too."

Hugo's nerves were at an all-time high as they made their way around the corner to Erin's. What if they ran into someone they knew? What if Dad was at work and realized he needed more papers to put inside his briefcase, so he went back home and realized Hugo wasn't there? Humans were always forgetting their papers! Hugo continued to worry about all the many, many ways he could get caught until they were standing below the side window of Erin's house.

Hugo helped Lulu climb onto an air-conditioning unit and then hopped up to join her. The window was open, and the only thing separating them from the inside of Erin's house was the screen. They peered into the laundry room and saw King sitting on the floor. He had a big plastic cone around his neck, and he looked so sad—sadder than Hugo had ever seen his friend. Lulu tapped the window screen with her paw and called out, "King! Hey, King!"

King turned toward the window and perked up slightly when he saw them. "Oh, hey!" he said. "What're you two doing here?"

"We're here to see you, silly!" shouted Lulu.

"How's your paw?" asked Hugo.

"It's just a cut," explained King, glancing down at his paw and looking sad again. "The vet put some sting-y stuff on it to keep it clean, and then put this cone around my neck so I can't lick it. Now I'm stuck here while Cleo gets to have a good time at the agility contest, and I can't even do anything fun like bite my own butt."

"That sounds like a bummer, King," said Hugo.

"It sure is," replied King. "I also can't exercise for a whole week!"

"That really stinks," Hugo said, trying to comfort King, who was looking more depressed by the second.

King nodded sadly. "But not in the good way, like grass with pee on it."

"Yeah. But you'll be good as new before you know it!" Hugo said with a smile. "One time, Enrique fell off his bike and broke his arm, and was in a cast for *weeks*. But I took good care of him, and he was back to riding his bike and playing soccer in no time! He didn't ask me to sign his cast, but that's okay, I'm not even holding a grudge. I mean, I had been practicing my signature—a muddy paw print—but again, I'm not holding a grudge."

"It sounds like you are," said Lulu.

"Nope, no grudge here," insisted Hugo.

"It really does sound like it, though."

"Enough!" squeaked King. "Hugo, that's a nice story, but I don't deserve to have anyone take care of me. Not now. Not ever. It's probably for the best that I'm locked up in the laundry room with a big cone around my neck. It'll keep me from ever being a bad dog again."

"You're not a ba—" Hugo began, but King cut him off.

"I *am*," he shouted. "I'm a bad dog! I'm a very, very bad dog who did a very, very bad thing. Cleo made that super clear last night. I bet as soon as she and Erin get back from the contest, they'll return me to the shelter."

Hugo's ears hung low with sympathy. He had never spent any time in a dog shelter, so he didn't know what they were like, but he was certain that once you got to a home, you wouldn't want to go back.

Poor pup, he thought. *He seems really upset.*

Lulu had far less sympathy. "Stop being such a drama queen," she snapped. "Or a drama *King*!"

"I'm neither," King moaned. "I just really pooped on it this time, and now Erin will be mad at me forever! Even though all I want in my *life* is to show her how much I love her! She's the best human in the world! She's perfect! She's incredible! And have you *smelled* her?! Oh my dog! There's no one better than Erin! Oh, Erin, what have I done!"

King started howling, and Hugo looked around nervously, certain they were about to get caught.

"Okay, kid, you need to calm down," said Lulu. "We get it, Erin is great! But it's time to cheer up, because we're here to spring you! If you come with us, we can take the cone off and everything! A cone is *not* fashion, no matter how hard you try to *make* it fashion. Trust me, I know from experience."

King just turned his back to them, lay down on the floor, and sighed heavily.

"How about we go to the park?" Lulu tried, but King didn't budge. He just looked even more upset.

Hugo turned to Lulu. "He doesn't want to come. It's probably too hard to revisit the place where it all happened. Maybe this is a good opportunity to go back home. No harm, no foul. We've had a nice walk."

"Don't give up so fast. I have an idea," Lulu whispered in Hugo's ear. Then she turned back to the window. "Hey, King! If we go to the park, maybe we could find Erin's scarf! How could she possibly be mad at you if you brought her scarf back?"

King's tail started wagging. When he turned around, his eyes were big and excited. "Genius!" he yelped, and he started running around in little circles. He clearly liked this idea a lot. He looked pretty silly running around with the cone on his head, and Hugo started laughing. Lulu, meanwhile, lifted the window screen with one of her carefully manicured, sparkly nail-arted paws and King was suddenly free. He leapt across the room and climbed onto a hamper, and with one big jump he was out the window.

Welp, thought Hugo, *there's no going back now.* He thought of the dog in a movie he'd watched with his family the week before—she got separated from her owners and spent years wandering through the wilderness, making friends with wild animals, always trying to find her owners. *That's us now,* Hugo mused. *No home, no responsibilities—we're all on the lam.*

Then he chuckled quietly, imagining himself sitting on a lamb—*so funny*—as he hopped off the air conditioner and they made their way toward the park, no leashes in sight.

CHAPTER 4

*S*CARF, SCARF, SCARF, *gotta find the scarf, grass, bird! Focus, King! You're looking for a scarf!*

King's mind raced as he, Lulu, and Hugo desperately searched the area around the fountain for Erin's scarf. King was a dog on a mission: If he could find the scarf and bring it back to Erin in mostly one piece, maybe she would forgive him for splashing around in the fountain yesterday. He would do anything to make up for misbehaving.

Sure, today he had escaped from his house through a window and was now running around the park unaccompanied, but this time he was misbehaving for a very good reason! Plus, it was early morning, so barely any people were around.

Where are you, scarf? Where are you? Ooh—what's that?! Nope, just some grass. Grass! Maybe I could go smell it! No, King! Focus!

Just then, a familiar voice called out to them. "Oh, thank goodness you're here! I need your help!"

King, Lulu, and Hugo looked up to see Nuts the squirrel pacing anxiously on the edge of the fountain.

"I've lost my acorns again!" Nuts exclaimed. "Can you help me find them?"

"Did you check under the elm tree?" Lulu replied, rolling her eyes.

"No. Why would I check under the—" Nuts began, but Lulu interrupted.

"We could actually use *your* help, Nuts! Have you happened to see a red-and-blue scarf in the park? The one Erin was wearing yesterday?" Lulu gave her best sympathetic smile. "We'd really appreciate the help of a great friend like you . . ."

"Oh yes! I saw it right here, in the grass near the fountain last night. It was so silky and cozy that I wove it into my nest! Is that what it's called? A *scarf*? Huh! I've been calling it a perfect squirrel mattress!"

"We're going to need that back," said Lulu.

"But . . . ," Nuts started, his floofy tail deflating. "I had the best sleep of my life last night. That thing is incredible. I usually have all this back pain, and my posture—and you know, a good night's sleep can really affect your whole day, and—anyways, it's mine now."

"Actually, it's Erin's!" King replied defiantly. "And I need to get it back to her. It was a birthday present!"

"A birthday present?" repeated Nuts. "Why would someone give a *person* a squirrel mattress for their birthday?"

King huffed impatiently, and Nuts paused, softening a bit. "Look, I'm sorry," he said. "It's a real shame she lost it. But aren't you all familiar with the Golden Rule of the park? It's been passed down for generations . . ."

"Yes, of course," Hugo answered wisely. "If it's golden, someone already peed there."

"No," said Nuts. "The other Golden Rule."

"Look both ways before you run around in a circle?" Lulu tried.

"No! The *other* other Golden Rule," said Nuts. "*Finders Keepers!* So there, it's settled, the so-called 'scarf' is mine, we're all in agreement, and speaking of finding things, I *really* need to find my acor—"

But King had heard enough. They were there for one thing and one thing alone—to get Erin's scarf back—and he wasn't about to let a squirrel get in his way. He lunged toward Nuts, crouching low to the ground and getting right in his face. Then he let out his fiercest puppy growl. "I need that scarf!" he barked. "It's Erin's! I will defend her until I die!"

Nuts stared at him in shock, then looked to Lulu and Hugo for support. "A little help here, folks?" he asked. "Can dogs put other dogs on leashes or . . ."

"Sorry, Nuts," Lulu replied. "But for one of the first times since I've known him, King is right. We need to get that scarf back."

"And . . . what if I don't give it to you?" Nuts asked, slowly backing away from King.

"Well then," Lulu replied. "We'll have no choice but to . . ."

She glanced at Hugo, then King, then back to Nuts. "Chase you," she said.

Hugo gasped. King gasped. Nuts stared at Lulu, wide-eyed.

"*Chase* me? Come on. We're all friends here, you three are good dogs, and you'd never—"

Lulu interrupted him with a loud growl—a sound King had never heard from her before—and leapt toward Nuts. King followed her lead, and just like that, the chase was on!

Nuts zipped and zoomed around the park as Lulu and King ran after him, a gleam in their eyes. Hugo hesitated for just a moment, looking around to make sure there weren't any disappointed humans watching, then joined in.

All three dogs were sprinting as fast as they could

as the sprightly squirrel dashed through bushes, under benches, and into the dog run, trying his best to lose them. Nuts was fast, but a bit out of practice, and King, Lulu, and Hugo managed to catch up with him at every turn.

Finally, Nuts must have realized there was one place the dogs couldn't reach him, and he scurried up a tree, hiding among its thick branches. Lulu, Hugo, and King gathered at the trunk, barking up toward the scarf-stealing squirrel, trying to get him to come back down. Instead, he jumped to another tree, and the dogs followed. This continued for a while, Nuts jumping from tree to tree and the dogs following underneath.

King felt exhilarated. "Is this what chasing squirrels always feels like?" he yelped.

"I think so," Hugo replied. "I don't really remember . . . It's been a while."

"I think it probably depends on the squirrel," Lulu said. "But you're right. This is great!"

"Why doesn't Erin let us do this?" King continued. "Maybe she doesn't know how FUN it is and how GOOD it feels! She should really try chasing a squirrel."

After what felt like an eternity of running, the dogs trapped Nuts in a tree that was at the end of the line.

Out of breath, Nuts looked defeated and ready to throw in the towel or, in this case, the scarf.

"All right. You got me. This happens to be the tree where I built my nest, and if you three aren't going to get tired any time soon, then I don't have much choice," he said. He removed the scarf from his nest and held it over the dogs' heads, ready to drop. "Here you go. Goodbye, perfect squirrel mattress."

Nuts dropped the scarf from the branch above them, and all three dogs leapt for it at once.

"I got it!"

"No, I got it!"

"Mine! Mine! I got it!"

King, Lulu, and Hugo all excitedly caught the scarf in their mouths, pulling in opposite directions, and then—RRRIP!—King heard the sound of the scarf shredding apart. Then another RRRIP! And another. Just like that, the scarf was in pieces.

"Oh no," whimpered King.

"Serves you right," yelled Nuts, retreating safely into his nest.

King whined sadly, looking down at the torn scraps of the scarf. "If Erin loved one normal-sized scarf, maybe she'll love a bunch of tiny scarves even more?" he wondered softly, but deep down he knew this was a disaster.

"It's okay," said Lulu. "Maybe we can fix it."

She gathered some mud and tried sticking the pieces back together with it, but it was no use—now they were just looking at a muddy torn-up scarf.

"You're making it worse," pointed out King. "She can't see it like this! It would be better if it was lost forever! We need to hide these pieces! Bury them! What if Erin brings us here tomorrow and sees what's left of her scarf? She could sniff out that we were involved!"

"She won't be able to smell that," Lulu reminded him gently. "Human noses are just for decoration."

"BURY BURY BURY!" King snapped. "We have to bury the pieces! Now now now!"

"Okay, okay!" said Lulu. "But if you're gonna dig, you'll need to take that cone off."

"But if Erin sees me without the cone . . ."

"She won't," assured Hugo. "It's all right, buddy. We'll put it back on you right after we get cleaned up."

Hugo pulled off the cone with his teeth, and the dogs hid it in the bushes. Then it was time to dig.

"Well," Lulu said, looking down at her body. "If I'm dressed like a dog today, might as well act like one. For a good cause. Let's split up and spread out." And they did, each taking a few pieces of scarf to bury.

Dirt, dirt, dirt! Hole, hole, hole! Rock! Stick! Dirt, dirt, dirt! Digging holes was fun! Almost as fun as chasing that squirrel, King thought as he dug and dug and dug. No! Even more fun!

Lulu and Hugo were also having a great time digging their holes. By the time they were all done, they had way more holes than they needed to bury the scarf pieces.

"Hey, Nuts!" Lulu called up into the tree. "You can use some of these extra holes to hide your acorns, if you want!"

Nuts just huffed.

"Don't worry, he'll get over it," Lulu said to King and Hugo. But King started whimpering again. After finishing the holes, he started thinking . . .

"Lulu? Hugo? I just had a terrible thought. Are we being . . . *bad*?" King asked softly.

Lulu and Hugo exchanged a look, unsure how to respond.

"It kind of feels like we're being bad . . . We're not bad dogs, are we?" King asked, looking down at the ground, embarrassed.

Hugo sighed and nodded sympathetically at King before looking back to Lulu. "I was wondering the same thing," Hugo said. "I mean, I have to admit . . . the chasing and the digging felt pretty amazing. It was more playing than I've done with my family lately . . . but what would our owners think about all of this?"

Lulu looked away, a flash of guilt in her expression. But it faded quickly, and she turned back to them with confidence. "Don't be ridiculous. Hugo, we *had* to get you away from the *thing*, right?"

Hugo didn't answer.

"And then we *had* to come here and look for the scarf," she continued. "When Nuts wouldn't give it back . . . we had no choice but to chase him! We've only done what we've had to do!"

Hugo nodded slowly. "Yeah, you're right," he said, his eyes lighting up. "We're not bad dogs. We're just good dogs having a bad day!"

"Exactly," said Lulu, nodding. "Happens to the best of us."

King smiled. "Thank goodness," he said. "Of course we're good dogs. You're right. Should we call it a day and— Oh no!"

He was suddenly distracted by his own paws, which were supposed to be white, but just then were caked in dirt and mud. Then he looked at Lulu and Hugo, who had gotten even messier than him! Lulu had grass and twigs all over her usually perfect fur. Hugo's entire mouth and nose were covered in the dirtiest dirt, like he'd been digging face-first.

"We're all filthy!" said King. "We can't go home like this. I mean, I think we smell delicious. Mud, grass, *and* drool? Mmm, mmm, mmm. But our humans would think we stink."

"Don't worry," Hugo replied. "We just need to get wet somehow, to clean off! Whenever I'm messy, Mom and Enrique give me a big bath . . . If only there was a big bath in the park . . ."

"Well . . . ," Lulu said. "Are you two looking at the same thing I'm looking at?"

"Oh my goodness. Yes, I am," said Hugo.

"That delicious-looking stick over there?" asked King, panting excitedly as he looked at a stick. "Those don't make you cleaner. If they did, I'd be spotless."

"No, King. *That.*"

King followed Lulu's gaze to see what they were staring at: the fountain. In all its wet, splashy glory.

Should they . . . ?

CHAPTER 5

THIS IS, IN its own way, a bit like going to the spa, thought Lulu as she let the cool water from the fountain rain down and cover her body from head to toe.

Come to think of it, the spa should install a fountain you can run around in! You are just full of brilliant ideas, Lulu, Lulu thought. *Yes I am, Lulu,* she also thought. *Yes I am.*

She'd been playing in the fountain with King and Hugo for what felt like a hundred dog minutes. What had started as a way to quickly clean their paws had turned into a total splash-fest!

"Look, look! What am I?" King asked excitedly, rolling around in the water.

"I don't know, what?" Hugo replied.

"A really, really wet puppy!" King exclaimed.

Lulu laughed and gave herself a good shake,

splashing King and Hugo and making them laugh even more.

Then, from behind them, they heard a loud human voice, getting closer.

"Dogs! Dogs in the fountain!" the human voice cried out.

Dogs?! Where?! thought Lulu, craning her head around to look.

The human got closer, and she did not look happy. She waved for them to get out of the water.

"Get out of there! Go on! Out! Where are your owners?!"

"It seems she's talking about *us*," Lulu said, annoyed, as she hopped out of the fountain, King and Hugo following close behind her. But then she looked down at her wet fur and realized that she did, today especially, look like a dog. And she was surprised to find that she didn't exactly mind.

All three dogs shook wildly, drying their fur and soaking the angry woman, which only made her angrier. Then they ran across the lawn as far away from her as they could get.

"Phew! Close one," Lulu said as they settled down, far from the fountain. It was later in the morning now, and there were more people in the park. "Do you think we should wait over here until that woman leaves, and then go back over to the fountain and . . . you know . . . clean off our paws more?"

But her friends weren't listening. They were too busy staring at something. But what? Lulu followed their eyes to see a little boy holding an ice cream cone. Oh boy. Now Lulu was staring too.

"An ice cream cone . . . ," drooled Hugo.

"And not just an ice cream *cone*," said King, his mouth watering too. "There's also ice cream on top of it."

"Well, yeah . . . ," replied Hugo. "You know, when my kids were younger, we used to go down to Creamie's all the time, and they'd let me have my own doggy scoop. Banana peanut butter with marshmallows."

Lulu squealed with delight.

"We haven't done that in a while . . . ," Hugo continued, trailing off.

"Maybe the kid really wants to share," King offered.

"He looks like he's about four years old," said Hugo. "Sofia used to share her food with me all the time when she was that age."

Ice cream was a delicacy that Lulu rarely got to enjoy. It made her a bit bloated and gassy. But on a hot day like today, those dripping scoops sure looked delicious . . . And without Jasmine around, who would care if she got a little gassy?

The little boy's mother was nearby, fussing over a smaller girl, trying to buckle her into a stroller. She didn't notice the three dogs slowly moving closer to her son. Lulu, Hugo, and King approached him carefully, giving him their best puppy-dog eyes.

But the boy yanked his ice cream cone away from them and held it higher in the air. "Stinky woof-woofs!" he yelled.

Lulu gasped. *Who is he calling stinky?* she thought. *If he thinks I'm stinky now, he should wait until after I eat his ice cream and have gas all over this park!*

But then she regained her composure and realized something. She turned to King and Hugo. "He doesn't have to *give* us the cone," Lulu pointed out. "As soon as he lowers it, we'll be able to reach it ourselves. He's a very, very small human."

Hugo's eyes widened as King struggled to contain his drool.

"I don't know," said Hugo. "Is that really such a good idea? That sounds like . . . *stealing.*"

"Don't think of it as stealing," Lulu replied. "Think of it as helping."

King nodded slowly, thinking it over. "That *is* a lot of ice cream for such a little kid . . . ," he agreed, staring at the dripping ice cream cone, which the little boy had brought back down to mouth level. "If he gets a tummy ache, and we *could* have done something to help but we *didn't* . . . ? We'd regret it for the rest of our lives."

"Well, when you put it like that . . . ," said Hugo.

Lulu nodded. Then she took another step toward the boy, stood up on her hind legs, and snatched the cone away as fast as she could!

The boy immediately started sobbing. "Mooooom!!! Moooommmmy!!!" he cried.

Lulu stopped for a moment, feeling a sudden pang of regret. She considered letting go of the ice cream, barking an apology, and forgetting the whole thing.

But that feeling passed quickly, replaced by her much stronger desire to go to town on some ice cream. Horrified and thrilled at the same time, the dogs all bolted toward the other side of the park. When they were safely out of sight of the boy and his mother, they dug in, slobbering with joy as the sweet, sweet taste of cold, refreshing vanilla slushed around in their mouths.

"This is one of the greatest T-R-E-A-T-S I've ever had," said King, licking his lips.

"It's even better than I remembered," Hugo said. "Did they change ice cream to make it more delicious?"

As they licked up the last of it, Lulu realized that she was incredibly sticky. Her face, her paws . . . She'd gotten ice cream everywhere.

"I feel sticky behind my ears . . . How did I get ice cream back *there*?" said Hugo.

"My *butt* is sticky," said King. "But then again, my butt is always a little sticky."

"Wow, we ate that fast," said Lulu, looking down at the spot in the grass where the ice cream used to be. And that's when King started whining again.

"What's wrong?" Hugo asked.

"It's just . . . ," King started. "Erin says that good dogs NEVER steal people food."

"So what?" Lulu said, trying to sound sure of herself. "Erin's not here!"

"But Erin says that good dogs *always* act like good dogs, even when Erin isn't watching." King put his tail between his legs. "You guys . . . I think we're . . . *bad*. I think we're being bad dogs."

Lulu couldn't think of a response. *Are we bad?* she wondered. They *had* just stolen a little boy's ice cream cone, after all . . .

But then Hugo piped up. "Don't be silly, King. We're not bad, we're just . . ." Hugo trailed off, unable to think of an argument, then looked down at his paws, ashamed. "I don't know."

"But! But!" Lulu started. "That little boy was *rude* to us, and . . ."

King and Hugo both tilted their heads as if to say, "Really?"

Lulu thought for a moment. Chasing a squirrel, getting wet in a fountain, stealing ice cream . . . What would her Instagram followers say if they saw her today? She would *not* want to read those comments. And what would *Jasmine* say?

Well, Jasmine's not here, she thought. *If Jasmine had been paying attention to me instead of her audition, none of this would be happening.*

"Okay, fine," said Lulu. "Maybe some of the things we've done are a little bit, kind of, sort of, when you look at it in a certain way . . . *bad*. But so what?! Do you know how hard it is to be Hashtag Perfect all the time?"

"What's a hashtag? Is it a kind of breakfast?" asked King.

"What I'm trying to say is . . . all three of us work hard all the time to be good! And do our owners care? Do they appreciate us? Do they *thank* us for how good we are? No, no, and no! They aren't even spending time with us today! So maybe it's time to do things a little differently."

King was speechless. He looked scared.

Hugo paused, thinking for a moment, before responding. "I don't know about all of that . . . My family loves me," he said softly.

Lulu wasn't sure where her burst of confidence came from—maybe it was a sugar rush from the ice cream—but she kept going with it. "Sure they do, Hugo! But even so, they left you all alone today . . . at home, by yourself, with the *thing*! Is that a family that really appreciates their dog?"

Hugo whined. Lulu had struck a nerve.

King piped up, "But Erin only left me alone today because I was bad yesterday. If she finds out about today, I'll be in even more trouble."

"That's exactly it!" said Lulu. She was pacing in circles around them now. "We're *already* going to be in trouble! Running away from home, playing in the fountain, chasing a squirrel, stealing ice cream. So why not keep going, just a little bit? Why not have just one day of living it up, and having the best time? We act like good dogs every day! Can't we have one day where we just act like *dogs*?"

Hugo hesitated, then nodded slowly.

Lulu looked at King. "Remember how you felt yesterday, jumping into the fountain? Before you got in trouble."

"Those were forty-seven incredible seconds," said King.

"That's what I'm talking about," said Lulu. "What if you could have a whole *day* like that?"

"A . . . day?" said King.

"Seven dog days, if that's how you prefer to count."

"Wow," said King, a faraway gleam in his eyes. He thought for a moment, then looked back to Lulu. "Okay. But when we're done, we have to clean up and put my cone back on. Erin doesn't have to know about any of this."

"Of course," said Lulu, extending her paw out to the others. "It'll be our secret."

"Okay," said King, putting his paw on top of hers.

"Okay," said Hugo, adding his to the stack of paws.

"Okay," said Lulu, grinning. The last time she'd felt this rebellious was when she'd dressed up in a leather jacket (vegan, of course) for a photo shoot.

"Look who it is!" said Hugo, and Lulu and King turned to see a familiar figure strutting across the lawn. A black bulldog, digging around in a poor human's picnic basket and grabbing a sandwich before being chased away. *Napoleon!*

As he moved closer, King nervously called out to him. "Hello! Hi! Napoleon! Hello!"

Napoleon looked them all up and down, confused.

"I'm King," said King. "This is Lulu, and Hugo. Remember us? From yesterday?"

"Sort of . . . ," replied Napoleon, looking from one to the other.

"You stole my owner's scarf. I followed you into the fountain. Everyone was yelling. Remember?!"

"Oh yeah . . . sure," said Napoleon, not seeming that interested. "Sorry. That's, like, basically every day for me." He scanned the park for other snacks, but he didn't walk away.

"What are you doing here?" asked Lulu. "Where are your people?"

"The world is my people, princess," Napoleon replied. "I hopped the fence and came here without my human. I do it all the time."

Lulu, King, and Hugo exchanged looks. Napoleon was so confident, it made them feel scared and impressed at the same time.

"What are *you* all doing here?" asked Napoleon. "Aren't you part of that . . . Goody Two-Shoes Doggy Kindergarten? Is that what it's called? Where's the woman with the delicious scarf, and does she have another one? I'm hungry."

Lulu felt a bit insulted, but she wasn't sure why. "Actually, we're *also* here without our humans," she said. "We've decided to get a little bit . . . wild. Just for the day. We're not *always* good dogs. Today, we're *real* dogs."

"Yeah!" King said excitedly, wagging his tail. "Who cares what humans think, right?"

Hugo nodded in agreement.

Napoleon looked at them all skeptically. "Hmm . . . okay. Cool," he said. "So what kinds of wild and crazy things have you been up to so far?"

"So many!" said Lulu. "We chased a squirrel. We tore up a scarf. We dug a bunch of holes."

"We stole an ice cream cone," said Hugo.

"And we jumped in the fount—" started King, but Napoleon interrupted.

"That's cute," he scoffed, unimpressed. "But if that's your idea of wild, I feel sorry for you. That's just a typical Tuesday morning for me. If that's all I did, I'd be considered a very good boy."

Lulu opened her mouth to respond, but Napoleon continued.

"If you three *really* want to be *real* dogs for a day . . . if you really don't care what people think . . . I could show you a thing or two."

Lulu, Hugo, and King shared a nervous glance.

"Okay, sure! Show us what *real* dogs do," said Lulu, trying to play it cool.

"First off," Napoleon said as he started to walk across the lawn, the dogs following his cue, "you've done everything there is to do in this park. You'll have to start by coming *downtown* with me."

"Downtown?" asked Hugo. "But that's all the way . . . downtown."

"Isn't that where *people* are? Like, a LOT of people?" asked King in a hushed tone.

Napoleon nodded with a naughty smirk. "If a dog misbehaves," he said, "and no human is around to see it . . . did they really misbehave at all?"

"Whoa," said Lulu. Then she, King, and Hugo just stared at one another, stumped by this deep question. They were walking toward the exit of the park now.

"If you really want to live your best dog life . . . ," Napoleon called to them over his shoulder as he stepped outside of the park, "follow me!"

The other three dogs all took a deep breath, and then . . . they followed him.

CHAPTER 6

FREEDOM! THIS WAS all King could think as he ran through the streets of his neighborhood, trying to catch up with Hugo and Lulu, who were both trying to catch up with Napoleon.

Running around these streets without Erin and Cleo felt so . . . *different.* He could stop and sniff anything he wanted! He could pee *anywhere!* He could stop and sniff his own pee! He had done this fifteen times, and they had only been running for two blocks.

"Isn't life more fun without anyone telling you what to do?" Napoleon asked over his shoulder. "Owners can be so strict and stuffy. You were meant to be wild and free!"

Maybe life is more fun without anyone telling me what to do, King thought, licking a dirty rock. He realized he was standing on a forbidden front lawn—Mr. Dunphy's house—and it felt great.

"Hey! Check it out! I'm eating Mr. Dunphy's grass!" he called out through a mouthful of grass. Usually Erin would tug hard on his leash when he got near this house, and Cleo would scold him if he thought about eating grass. But not today. "This is awesome!"

There was so much to see and so much to smell and so much to chew on that King almost felt like his brain might explode as he ran to catch up with his friends. If any humans were watching, King wondered what they would think. Would they be concerned to see four dogs running around the neighborhood off leash?

Nah! King decided. *They'll probably be happy and inspired, seeing a group of friends living their best life!*

But then—he heard a familiar voice.

"Well, well, well . . ."

King shivered, and the dogs stopped next to a tall wooden fence.

Uh-oh, thought King. He would recognize that voice anywhere . . . He even heard it in his nightmares.

"If it isn't shelter inmate number 71245," the silky voice purred from a tree above them. "Running around off leash, I see. I'm not surprised. You know your human didn't *mean* to adopt a goofball mutt like you, right?"

It was King's nemesis. Pickle the cat.

He whined and cowered underneath the tree, then looked up to see her face peering down at him. Pickle was perched on a high branch, looking smug as ever.

The dogs passed by Pickle's house every day on their way from Good Dogs to the park, and every day she had something new and nasty to say to them from her tree. Usually they just ignored her, since Erin was around. But today they were alone.

"It's just a matter of time," said Pickle, "before Erin realizes it and sends you back to the shelter."

King wished he still had the cone on, so that it could block out the sound of Pickle's hurtful words. She had a way of figuring out each dog's worst fear. King wondered if she just sat up there all day, thinking of mean things to say. Pickle glanced from King to Lulu, Hugo, and Napoleon, who had also stopped in the shade of the tree.

"Maybe you'll be able to share a cell with these two," Pickle said, gesturing to Hugo and Lulu. "This one's family would rather have a puppy, and this one doesn't realize she's just her owner's Instagram meal ticket."

"Pickle!" shouted Hugo. "Stop saying those terrible things!"

But King could tell Pickle had gotten to Hugo, whose ears drooped down as he looked away from the other dogs.

"Sorry," said Pickle, but King knew she wasn't. "I'm a cat. I can't help being smarter than all of you. And more lovable. And cleaner. Way cleaner. And less . . . slobbery. Also quieter. Longer life span. I could go on. And I will! Less smelly. Smarter. Did I say that already? Better at taking care of myself. I don't need day care like you dogs. More interested in faucets—"

"Enough!" snapped Lulu. Then she turned to King, Hugo, and Napoleon. "She's a bully. Let's just keep walking and ignore her."

And so the dogs started to walk away. Except for Napoleon, who lingered underneath the tree and called after them. "Hold up," he barked. "Are you just going to let a cat talk to you like that?"

"What choice do we have?" asked Hugo. "Maybe she is smarter and cleaner and more lovable than us . . . I don't know."

"She's definitely meaner than us," Lulu said under her breath.

"Yeah, but we're bigger," said Napoleon. And then he did something really gutsy. He walked over to the base of Pickle's tree and bumped the trunk as hard as he could with his butt.

The branches shook! Caught off guard, Pickle let out a loud, terrifying yowl and fell to the ground outside of the tall wooden fence. She fell on her paws, of course, but now she was trapped.

"Uh-oh," she said, looking around. "I'm supposed to be in the backyard! This is . . . the *front* yard!"

"She's off her home turf," yelled Napoleon to the other dogs. "Show her who's boss! Or . . . are you three too *well behaved*?"

King watched as Lulu slowly, hesitantly approached Pickle. The cat crouched down, flattened her ears, and hissed.

Lulu cleared her throat and gave Pickle a very stern look. "I do not care for your attitude!" she barked confidently. "Not one bit! This may sound harsh, Pickle, but if you followed me on Instagram, I would *not* follow you back!"

Lulu wagged her tail proudly as if she'd won the battle. But that's when Pickle pounced, letting out a loud shriek and slashing at Lulu with her claws, narrowly missing. King ran to Lulu's side to help his friend, and Hugo did too.

"Why would I care what a silly floofball like you thinks?" said Pickle, getting in Lulu's face. "You might think you're special, but it's only a matter of time before your human gets a big role on a TV show, and then she'll get too busy to take care of you. Buh-bye! You'll be the most famous dog at the shelter!"

"So then we agree on one thing," Lulu said. "Jasmine is very talented!"

Then Lulu summoned a booming growl that made everyone's head turn. It was even louder and deeper than the sound she'd made in the park to scare Nuts, King thought. She advanced on Pickle, flanked by King and Hugo, and Pickle retreated nervously toward the fence.

The cat gave one last big swat at Lulu's face, with her claws extended, then darted off as fast as she could, yelling as she went. "BATHTUB! HALLOWEEN COSTUME! BALLOONS!"

"What's she yelling about?" King whined softly.

"Shh... Those are cat swear words," Hugo explained.

"CUCUMBERS! LOUD NOISES! NEW PEOPLE!" Pickle continued cursing as she ran off.

"That was great!" Napoleon said. "See? Don't you feel better? You don't need to let some *cat* push you around."

King thought about it. He wasn't sure if he felt better, or just ... different. And he couldn't get what Pickle had said out of his mind. Would Erin really send him back to the shelter if he wasn't good?

Lulu licked her nose. "Ouch. I think she scratched me with that last swipe," she said. "My perfect nose, scratched? What will my followers think?"

"Oh, that'll heal fast," said Napoleon reassuringly. "And besides, it's like I always say: You can't make a point without getting a few scratches on your nose."

"You *always* say that?" King asked.

"Hey, everyone," Hugo piped up as they followed Napoleon away from the house. "You think Pickle's gonna be able to get back into her yard?"

"I doubt it . . . ," Lulu said, and they turned back to see the frustrated cat trying and failing to climb the tall fence.

"And whose problem is that?" asked Napoleon. "Not mine, that's whose!"

"I'm just saying . . . she's very good at holding a grudge," said Hugo. Lulu and King nodded. "We'll definitely hear about this the next time we see her."

"Ah, don't worry about that!" Napoleon said, strutting confidently down the street. "We're dogs! She's a cat! Real dogs don't worry about what some *cat* thinks."

Whoa, thought King. *This guy's full of wisdom.*

"Real dogs don't worry about what some cat thinks . . . ," King repeated out loud, thinking about how wonderful it would be to truly believe that. He used to be terrified of Pickle's tree when he was walking with Erin, but today he'd fought back. King could feel his tail starting to wag.

"Yeah! Why *should* we let her get to us?" he said confidently.

"Because she has claws . . . ," Lulu replied softly, wiggling her nose.

Napoleon was getting farther ahead of them now, and he turned to call back to them. "Keep up! There's more to do, more to see, more to conquer!"

So Lulu, Hugo, and King broke into a run to catch up.

CHAPTER 7

I T WAS LATE in the morning now, and the hot sun was glaring down on them. It had been a while since Hugo had spent this much time outside. They were all panting to keep cool, especially Napoleon, whose pants were way louder and heavier than everyone else's. Hugo noticed that Napoleon's tongue flopped out of the side of his mouth and seemed to have an extra coat of slobber.

Wow, side tongue action! He even pants like a bad boy, Hugo thought as they followed Napoleon down the street. Then, suddenly, their leader stopped in his tracks and turned around.

"Can we swing by one of your houses to get some water?" Napoleon asked. Well, he didn't so much as ask as *demand*, but as a question. Hugo, Lulu, and King just stared at him, then at one another, then back at him. Hugo didn't want to offer up his home to someone as naughty and unpredictable as Napoleon, and he could tell the others felt the same way. Napoleon stared them each down, waiting for someone to cave. No one did.

"Oh, come on! What's a dog gotta do to get a drink around here?!" Napoleon asked. "Being bad makes me thirsty. So I'm *always* thirsty."

"Well, you can't come to my house," said Lulu, sticking up her nose. "There are too many delicate things there. Like my mechanical treat dispenser and my collection of antique porcelain dolls!"

"And we can't go to my house either," King said, thinking fast. "Because, uh . . . uh . . . I barfed in there earlier, and it smells real bad."

Hugo wasn't sure whether King was lying. Then Hugo thought about his own house. His wonderful, cozy home that was usually full of fun and laughter. Now it was being destroyed by the *thing*. No. They couldn't go there. Everyone would understand.

"Sorry," said Hugo. "We can't go to my house. The *thing* is there."

Napoleon looked at him curiously. "What *thing*?" he asked.

Hugo didn't want to say. It was too scary! But Napoleon wasn't going to let it go.

"What *thing*?" he asked again.

"It's hard to explain," Hugo said. "But the thing works

for my humans. It's a big circle that runs all around the house sucking stuff up like dirt and dust and my fur. It makes a lot of noise, like it's real angry all the time. I think it hates the floor and anything on it, especially paws."

To Hugo's surprise, Napoleon suddenly became angry! "And your humans put this . . . this *thing* in the house while you're *home*?! The nerve! They sound awful!"

Hugo suddenly felt bad. He hadn't meant to make his family seem like mean people. They weren't! He couldn't deny that the *thing* scared him, and that they had let it into his home. Still, he wanted to defend them.

"It's new! I think they just don't understand that I—"

"I've heard enough," Napoleon said definitively. "We're going to Hugo's house. I'm going to take a long drink of water. And then I'm going to tell that *thing* who's boss."

"Who *is* the boss?" asked Hugo.

"*You* are!"

Hugo's eyes widened. Could that be true? "Me? The *boss*? Are you sure?"

Napoleon seemed very sure. "The dog is always the king of the castle, Hugo," he said. "All you have to do is believe it. Now, where's your house?"

"His house is just up ahead," Lulu blurted out before Hugo could stop her. "To the left! It's the big brick one with the porch."

"But you can't get in," said Hugo. "There's a gate, and it's really hard to get open!"

But it was no use telling Napoleon what he could and couldn't do. The devious rascal was running ahead of them, and by the time they had all caught up, he had already figured out how to open the gate. He didn't even need a broomstick. It was clear he'd had a lot of practice breaking and entering.

"Please," Hugo pleaded, trying to bargain with Napoleon one last time. "I'll get you some water if you just leave the *thing* alone." But Napoleon wasn't listening. He was standing in the yard, watching the *thing* intently through the back windows. He uttered a low, guttural growl.

"This stops now," Napoleon announced, then darted through the doggy door and into the house. He let out a big howl and took a running leap toward the *thing*. Then he started whaling on it, attacking it with his front paws.

Hugo ran in after him. "Please, don't!" he shouted. "Stop! The *thing* might be terrible, but it belongs to my family!"

"You're a sweet dog," Napoleon said, speaking between big swings and bites as he systematically destroyed the *thing*. "It's nice of you to think of your humans, but did they think of *you* when they brought this *thing* into the house?! No!"

"Oh, come on! You don't even know them—" Hugo started to protest, but then he remembered that Lulu had said the same thing that morning, and she did know them.

Hugo whimpered and looked at the floor. Maybe Napoleon was right after all. His family used to plan their schedules around his walks. They had bought a special couch that he could sit on without messing up the fabric with his nails. Once they even took a driving vacation instead of a flying one so that Hugo could go with them! But those days seemed long gone now, and they had brought an evil *thing* into their home, *his* home, just to torment him! Noticing Hugo's expression, Napoleon nudged what was left of the *thing* a bit closer to him.

"Free yourself, man," Napoleon said. Then he pummeled the *thing* one more time with a swift kick. The *thing* let out a long whine full of beeps and buzzes, and suddenly Hugo was filled with an urge from deep within to end the *thing* once and for all. It felt like all of Hugo's dog ancestors, throughout all of time, all the way back to wolves, were telling him that the *thing* needed to go. That it was Hugo or the *thing*, and only one of them could survive.

Hugo raised his paw and brought it smashing down onto the *thing*. A rush of excitement came over him, and he jumped, attacking the *thing* from above.

This feels incredible, he thought. Soon he was hitting the *thing* left and right, up and down, and Napoleon was whooping and cheering him on.

"There you go! Feels good, huh? Nice one!" Napoleon barked excitedly. "Lulu! King! Join in on the fun! Go to town!"

Soon, all the dogs were beating on the *thing* and kept at it until it was barely a *thing* anymore. It had stopped moving or making sounds, and they were now tearing it apart and chewing it up into tiny, slobbery pieces. Hugo felt so excited! He did a victory lap around the house, wagging his tail and howling breathlessly.

When he came back, the attack had stopped. Lulu, King, and Napoleon stood around, looking at the pieces on the floor, surveying the damage. The *thing's* metal guts were strewn about the sunroom floor. It was not a pretty sight.

Hugo's stomach dropped, and he suddenly felt a lump in his throat. All the joy and elation he'd felt a moment earlier was replaced with panic and regret.

"Oh no," he said. "What have we done?"

Hugo always considered the number one house rule to be "respect the house." He even tried not to shed on the couch. It never worked, but at least he tried. And now he'd demolished something that belonged to his family!

"You did what needed to be done," said Napoleon. "Now the house is yours again! You can move around freely. Nothing can stop you."

But Hugo wasn't convinced. He was definitely happy that he'd never have to run away from the awful *thing* again, but he couldn't shake the feeling that, in destroying it, he'd also destroyed the trust of his family. He understood how King must have felt, staring at the torn pieces of Erin's scarf. He suddenly understood why King had been so desperate to hide the evidence, to make the problem disappear, like it had never even happened.

"Come on," said Hugo urgently. "We have to bury all the pieces. Like we did with the scarf! That way, when my family comes home, they'll just think the *thing* ran away! Like maybe it went to go live with its friends."

"You wanna bury the evidence? No problem. I know a guy," King said, trying to sound cool, but wagging his tail uncontrollably. "It's me. I'm the guy. I love digging! I'll do it."

"Don't be a fool, Hugo," said Napoleon sternly. "If you want to send a message to your humans, you gotta leave it all here for them to find. They need to see that they should never mess with you again. Or they'll have to face the consequences."

Hugo looked at him, unsure. He hung his head.

Napoleon continued. "Or, if you *really* want to send a message, you could pee in their shoes. Or barf on their bed. Or *eat* their shoes and then barf out the shoes on the bed. And *then* pee—"

"No thanks. Leaving the pieces out might be more my speed," said Hugo sadly.

"Good choice. Plus, we have more important things to do. Like get that drink I wanted. Where do you keep the water 'round here?"

Napoleon padded away, not toward the kitchen, where Hugo's water bowl was sitting, but straight to the bathroom. Hugo, Lulu, and King listened in shock as he lapped up water from the toilet. *Splash, splash, splash.* He just kept drinking and drinking.

"Uh-oh," King said. "If he drinks all your toilet water . . . there won't be any left for your family to drink!"

Before Hugo or Lulu could correct him, Napoleon emerged from the bathroom, licking his lips. "Ahh," he said. "There's nothing like drinking water straight from the source."

"I don't think—" Lulu started, but Napoleon was already across the room and halfway out the doggy door.

"You coming?" he asked them. "Our next stop is downtown. I'm your teacher. Today's lesson is How to Be Bad. And downtown is my classroom. You three have so much to learn. Let's go!"

With that, he was out the door. Hugo, Lulu, and King looked at one another hesitantly. Things were about to get pretty wild, that much was clear.

Part of Hugo just wanted to stay home and curl up on the couch with a good book to eat. But a bigger part of him wanted to see where this adventure would take them. He thought about his family. Maybe it was true that they'd stopped paying attention to him because he'd become less fun and spontaneous.

Well, he thought. *There's nothing more spontaneous than following a strange French bulldog downtown!*

CHAPTER 8

AS THE DOGS trailed after Napoleon, the streets got narrower and more crowded. Lulu had gone downtown with Jasmine loads of times, but she was usually being carried in a handbag or carrier. She'd never roamed the streets like this before, and it was exciting! Everywhere she looked there were cars and bikes and people and dogs! Everywhere she smelled there were new, strange smells. The smells of the *city*.

Lulu's days were usually so carefully scheduled that she didn't have time to stop and sniff a tree trunk or investigate a pee-covered rock. Now everywhere she looked, the world was full of possibilities. Brand-new paths were waiting to be discovered and explored!

What a wonderful afternoon, she thought as she and Hugo raced each other to a big stick and tugged

on opposite ends of it with their teeth. It was such a relief to not constantly ask herself, "What would a tiny, fancy person do?" or, "How would @LulusPerfectLife behave?" For once, she was just asking herself, "What do I want to do right now?"

King had excitedly stopped to pee, or to smell pee, ten times already on one block, and it looked like he was having a lot of fun, so Lulu started to do the same. As she peed on the sidewalk next to a mailbox, she thought about the other dogs who would come to this corner later, smell her pee, and know she had been there.

This is kind of like tagging your location on Instagram, she thought. *Only with more pee!* This must be how it felt to be a *real* dog, she figured. And it felt good.

But still, she did miss being carried. And her paws were getting pretty dirty.

Then they passed a storefront Lulu hadn't seen before, with a lot of pretty clothes in the window. Colorful sundresses, stylish boots, sparkly hats.

The humans in storefront windows are always so good at standing still, Lulu thought as she admired the outfits. This was exactly the kind of store Jasmine would take her to, buying an outfit for herself and a matching look for Lulu.

It wasn't quite the same, walking by a new store without her best friend.

She wondered what Jasmine was up to right now. It made her a little sad, not knowing, but then she remembered that Jasmine was the one who had left her alone this morning in the first place.

Probably regretting that she didn't take me with her today, Lulu thought.

They had just reached the main drag, full of bustling shops and restaurants, when Napoleon suddenly veered away from the sidewalk and led them into a back alley, stopping next to a big stinky dumpster.

"This better not be where we're having lunch," Lulu huffed.

"No way," replied Napoleon. "Today we eat like kings!"

Napoleon was shaking his head back and forth super fast and pawing at his neck.

What on earth, Lulu started to think, but when she saw Napoleon's collar slip off his neck and over his head, she realized what was going on.

"Come on," Napoleon said to the group. "You all do the same. Lose the collars."

"But then no one will know who we are," said Hugo.

"Where we're going, we don't want anyone to know who we are," Napoleon said, staring intensely into the distance.

♥. *Lulu*

Whoa, thought Lulu. *That's cool. But wait a second!* She had another thought.

"I might be recognized even without my tags," she said. "I'm a *very* famous Instagram celebrity. I was just on a *list* called '35 Very Good Dogs You Simply Must Follow, or Else.' Someone downtown might recognize me from one of my many critically acclaimed public appearances, like . . . the time I went to the dentist, or the time I went to the hardware store!"

"I can fix that," said Napoleon, and he proceeded to muss up Lulu's fur with his paws. There was an old broken mirror leaning against the dumpster, and he pushed it toward her so she could see her reflection. "See? Now you look like any old mutt from the pound."

She turned to look. At first she barked: There was another dog in the mirror! Then she realized it was just her. Which made her bark *even more*, because she looked so different. She pouted at her reflection. She was a mess! Her hair was going every which way, and she even had some mud on her face! But she had to admit, if only to herself, that there was something freeing about being in disguise. As much as she loved the facials and the grooming and the dog Pilates, it was kind of nice to have the afternoon off from living @LulusPerfectLife.

Napoleon grabbed all the collars in his mouth and hid them behind the dumpster.

King let out a little whine. "Goodbye, King," he said sadly to himself. "I'll miss you."

"You're still *King*," explained Lulu. "You just won't be wearing your collar."

"It's not the same," King whined again.

"It really is," Hugo muttered under his breath. "You have a microchip anyway."

"If anyone should be sad to lose their collar, it's me!" Lulu said. "Mine was engraved in calligraphy with my name, address, *and* social media handles. I bet it cost billions of dollars."

"Well," Hugo said. "Zoe made mine in preschool. It's irreplaceable."

"If you're all done whining about your collars, it's time to go," said Napoleon.

They fell in line behind Napoleon, and he led them farther down the alleyway, stopping outside the back door of a very fancy-looking shop.

"Behold," said Napoleon, a glimmer in his eye. "The Chic Patisserie. The crème de la crème of bakeries, the fanciest downtown. The stuff here is the real deal, and I would know, since I'm sort of French."

The dogs looked up at the door. King's stomach grumbled loud enough for all of them to hear. Lulu had always wanted to try this place's special treats . . .

"But they don't allow dogs," Lulu said. "Jasmine

takes me everywhere, but even *I've* never been inside the Chic Patisserie."

"Yeah, look," Hugo said, nodding toward a sticker on the door. It was an image of a dog with a line striking through it. "Seems pretty strict."

"You're right," King said, staring at the sign in terror. "That means if a dog goes in there . . . they put a *line through it.*"

"Have any of you ever tasted a delectable baked good from the Chic Patisserie?" Napoleon asked. The other dogs shook their heads. "Well then, today is your lucky day!"

"Are we going inside?" Lulu asked nervously, but with a tinge of excitement.

"Ha!" Napoleon laughed. "No. *Real* dogs eat what they want, when they want it, wherever they want it. Ta-da!"

He gestured behind them, and they all turned to look. Right behind them was a giant dumpster overflowing with treats from the bakery. Lulu's jaw dropped. It was so beautiful: Croissants, eclairs, macarons! An old dirty cup! Well, maybe that wasn't one of the treats . . . but everything else looked incredible.

"They put everything in here at the end of the day," Napoleon explained. "If we don't eat it, it'll just go to waste."

Then, without missing a beat, he jumped right in and started gorging on the fancy French treats. The other dogs looked at one another. None of them had ever eaten out of a dumpster before.

"Um . . . excuse me?" Lulu tried to get Napoleon's attention. "I specifically asked you if we were going to be eating out of a dumpster, and you said no."

Napoleon turned back to her with a mouth full of food. "No," he replied. "You asked me if we were going to be eating out of *that* one."

He gestured to the other dumpster, where they had hidden their collars. "We're eating out of *this* one. Now, if you'll excuse me . . ." Napoleon turned his attention back to his lunch.

"That *is* a fair point . . . ," King said with a shrug.

Lulu had eaten out of the trash when she was a puppy, but she'd sworn she would *never* make that mistake again. Cotton balls did *not* sit well in her stomach! But this was different. This dumpster was full of lavishly decorated, delicious-looking snacks, fit for a princess. And from the looks of it, most of these pastries hadn't been in the trash long. Some of them were still wrapped in beautiful white paper doilies that looked like snowflakes.

King jumped into the dumpster and immediately chomped down on an eclair, then Hugo joined him, and finally, so did Lulu. As soon as she sank her teeth into her first croissant, she knew she'd made the right decision. This was the most amazing food she'd ever eaten! She let out a few yelps of excitement and then a big howl. Napoleon, King, and Hugo followed suit, until they were all howling loudly with joy.

Lulu thought the only thing that could make this feast better would be if they were sitting inside at a table by the window, like the dignified canines they were. The more she thought about it, the more furious she became at the Chic Patisserie's strict no-dog policy. How *dare* they deprive her of such wonderful cakes and cream-filled treats?

Just then, the back door to the bakery swung open and an employee walked out, carrying a few trash bags. When he saw the dogs, he dropped the bags and grabbed a nearby broom.

"Get out of here, you mangy mutts!" he yelled, chasing them with the broom.

Lulu scoffed as they jumped out of the dumpster and ran away from the angry man. "Mangy mutt?" she said in disbelief when they were a safe distance away. "Jasmine spent forty-five minutes on my blowout this morning! I get my haircuts at a *very chic* salon!"

Then she remembered playing in the fountain and Napoleon mussing up her fur. *I guess I do look mangy,* she thought. She wasn't the only one offended. King was hanging his head in shame, Hugo was frowning, and Napoleon was snarling and running furiously in circles.

"'Mangy mutts'! That was out of line," he said. "Are we going to stand for that sort of language? That kind of *treatment*?! No! We have to do something!"

"What do you mean?" asked Hugo, whining.

"Let's just say, if you like their day-old stuff, just *wait* until you taste the fresh pastries," Napoleon said.

Hugo gasped. "You don't mean . . ."

"I do mean," Napoleon replied mischievously. "We're going inside."

They all looked over at the clean, fancy, *dog-free* bakery. The employee was gone now.

"We don't have our collars," Napoleon added. "No one will know who we are."

"It *was* rude of that human to call us mangy," added Lulu, warming up to the idea.

"Then follow me," Napoleon said, and ran back toward the door. The others followed close behind.

The employee had left the door propped open slightly, and Napoleon easily nudged it the rest of the way with his nose so the dogs could get through. They soon found themselves in a fancy kitchen. It smelled so good, but before Lulu could even take a full breath, the kitchen erupted in chaos.

"Dogs! Dogs!!! There are DOGS in the KITCHEN!"

Gosh, Lulu thought. *Humans can be so loud. Always yapping! They could really use some training . . .*

Someone screamed and dropped a tray of hot croissants, which bounced all around on the floor. A baker tried to grab Napoleon, who was leading the charge. But as the baker ran around the kitchen, he slipped on a buttery croissant and went flying through the air, landing in a giant bag of white flour. The bag exploded! Now the flour was absolutely everywhere, covering the kitchen staff, the dogs, the counters—everything—in a thick layer of powder. Suddenly the people looked like snowmen, and the dogs looked like . . . snowdogs.

The dogs ran out of the kitchen and into the front of the bakery, which, even amid the commotion, Lulu noticed was *very* fancy. It looked like a place she'd enjoy a lot, if she weren't being chased by a bunch of angry bakers with rolling pins.

A couple of kids started cheering, excited to see dogs, and Lulu noticed some young teenagers giggling uncontrollably as Hugo jumped up onto a nearby chair. But the rest of the bakery staff rushed into action. The cashier tried to catch them, but they ducked underneath tables, sped away from her, and ran around the counter in circles. Lulu barked—she felt alive! Sure, if Jasmine saw her right now, she'd be in a lot of trouble, but she was having *fun*! She watched as Napoleon grabbed a full baguette in his mouth and then ran toward the front door. She grabbed a blueberry scone for the road and followed him, darting behind a chair that had a bunch of chic silver balloons tied to it.

King and Hugo raced outside and joined them just as a baker came out the door waving a rolling pin wildly around over his head, shouting at the top of his lungs into a cell phone, "Animal control! I need animal control!"

They glanced at one another, and when Napoleon nodded, they all made a run for it. They kept running until the baker was far behind them. Napoleon, leading the herd, yelled back at them, "We have to wash away this evidence."

"Yes!" Lulu agreed. "We'll need a bath. A big one!"

"Back to the fountain?" Hugo asked, out of breath.

"That's too far," King pointed out. "It's all the way back at the park."

"I know just the place," Napoleon said, with a devious glint in his eye that was starting to look familiar. He led them around the corner and toward a big iron gate. Lulu knew immediately where they were: the public pool. The biggest bath in town.

Without thinking, Lulu followed Napoleon as he nudged the gate open, ran across a big patio full of kids, and then dove into the pool.

CHAPTER 9

Hugo

DOGS! DOGS IN the pool!" the lifeguards yelled, blowing their whistles.

It was utter chaos! There was yelling and splashing all around them as the dogs washed themselves off in the deep end. The pool was surrounded by a concrete deck, and beyond that, a grassy area with some tables and lawn chairs.

Hugo hadn't looked around much before they dove in, but now that he did, he could tell there was some kind of summer camp in session today, and the dogs had splashed right into the middle of it! Some kids scrambled out of the pool, while others jumped in and swam toward the dogs. Everyone was making a lot of noise, but Hugo hardly noticed the commotion because he was having so much fun.

He had forgotten that he could swim! Hugo was anxious jumping into the pool, but as soon as he hit the water, the memories came flooding back. Mom, Dad,

and Enrique used to take him to the lake when he and Sofia were both little. It had been a while, but now he was swimming again like no time had passed, and he was loving every minute of it.

"This feels amazing!" Hugo called out to the others as he freestyled around the cool, refreshing water of the deep end. "Nice doggy paddle, Lulu!"

"I call this a ME paddle!" Lulu replied. With her wet fur clinging to her body, Lulu looked about a quarter of her normal size, but she didn't seem to care. She looked like she was having the time of her life.

Most of the kids in the pool had human-paddled away from them now, leaving them more room to swim and have fun. In fact, Hugo noticed, they had the whole pool to themselves! One camp counselor tried to shoo them out but gave up, and the others were on the grass, trying to stop the campers from jumping back in. The lifeguards were all talking on their cell phones. One thing was clear: Everyone was watching them. The attention felt good. Hugo heard a few kids standing on the deck, pointing at them and laughing.

That's nice! Hugo thought. *We're making them laugh!* Normally Hugo wouldn't have just jumped into a pool full of people he didn't know, but he was starting to think that sometimes, maybe, acting wild and spontaneous could pay off. After all, those teens in the bakery had loved it when he'd run around and jumped up onto the chairs. *Maybe humans like it when I give in to my dog-giest instincts . . .*

"You guys wanna play Barko Polo?" Lulu asked.

"What's that?" King said.

"I close my eyes and you three swim around. When I bark, you bark back, and I try to find you and tag you!"

"That sounds fun," Napoleon said. "Let's play."

Lulu closed her eyes and barked loudly.

Hugo, King, and Napoleon barked in response. The dogs splashed around in the pool, playing their fun game until, suddenly, Hugo fell silent.

"Hold up. Does anyone else smell that?" Hugo asked with his snout up in the air, sniffing around for the source of a delicious scent. "It smells like . . ."

"SNACKS!" all the dogs barked in unison. Lulu's eyes popped open.

"There it is!" Napoleon said. He directed their attention to a table in the shady area of the grass, where an adult was putting out all kinds of treats—chips, candy, cookies, sandwiches, a stack of pizza boxes, and FRENCH FRIES!

"French fries!" Napoleon shouted. "The food of my people!"

Sure, Hugo had just filled up on amazing pastries from the trash, but when he thought about it, all the running around and chasing and breaking the *thing* and swimming *had* made him hungrier than usual.

So just like that, all four dogs climbed out of the pool, ran across the deck and onto the grass, and headed straight for the table.

"These are some of my favorite smells!!!" King cried out as they ran toward the snacks. "Did these humans know I was coming??"

"I don't think so, buddy," Hugo replied. "But they do now."

"Look out!" one of the humans yelled. "Here they come!"

"Really, Jason?" another one shouted. "You couldn't wait until after the dogs were gone to put out the food?!"

"I like Jason!" King yelled, his mouth watering.

The children and teenaged camp counselors dove out of the way as Hugo, Lulu, King, and Napoleon jumped onto the table and grabbed as many snacks as they could.

In the pandemonium, one of them—or maybe it was all of them, Hugo couldn't be sure—knocked over the table completely.

"The dogs are eating our snacks!"

Hugo was so busy eating that he didn't pay much attention to the humans for a few minutes. But when he came up from a bowl of barbecue potato chips, he noticed that something had changed. Now only a few of the kids were laughing. The others were yelling, running away, and he was stunned to see that some of them were even *crying*.

"What are we going to eat now?" one little girl whimpered. "When are these dogs going to stop?"

Hugo tried to lick the barbecue powder off his jowls as a horrible thought occurred to him: *Maybe we aren't making them happy after all. It seems like we're making some of them mad. Or worse,* scared!

"Guys?" he called out to the others. "Maybe we should settle down? I don't think these kids are very happy with us . . ."

Hugo noticed one boy in particular who had been laughing earlier, when the dogs were swimming in the pool. Now the boy had tears in his eyes and looked terrified.

Oh no, Hugo thought. *We've gone too far.*

King and Lulu both looked up from the pile of food, slowly noticing the same thing Hugo did. More kids were crying now, and the counselors were doing their best to comfort them. Lulu dropped the slice of pizza that was dangling from her mouth. She looked ashamed. Napoleon just shrugged them off and kept eating.

Then King noticed something, and his ears stood up on alert. "Look!" he yelped. "There's a humongous green dog over there!"

Hugo turned to see a huge alligator in the shallow end of the pool. It looked like it was frozen in place, and it was grinning right at them.

"King, that's not a dog. It's an alligator," Hugo pointed out. He loved to watch nature shows with his family on their shiny, flickering, funny rectangle, and he considered himself a bit of an expert on the different types of creatures in the world. *If Zoe was here*, Hugo thought, *she'd probably point at it and say, "Gatorgator!"* The thought made him miss snuggling up next to her on the couch.

But Hugo had never seen an alligator quite like this before. It was poofy, and colorful, and floating perfectly still in the pool with a big smile on its face.

Must be native to this part of the city, Hugo thought.

"An alligator?" King asked. "Is that a kind of cat? Sounds dangerous. Should we get out of here?"

"Wait!" Lulu barked excitedly. She looked like she had an idea. "Maybe it's not us making the humans upset . . . Maybe it's the alligator!"

Hugo thought about this. It made sense. "And if we scare the alligator away," he added, "that makes us heroes! They can't be mad at us anymore." If the campers were scared of some dogs, they were probably even more scared of an alligator! If they frightened the alligator away, they'd be protecting the humans, and that was *always* a good thing to do.

"Let's do it," Hugo said. Napoleon dropped his snacks and joined them, sensing a new adventure in the works.

"Are alligators afraid of dogs?" King asked.

"Only one way to find out," Napoleon said.

So they ran back toward the pool and splashed into the shallow end.

"Please leave the pool, alligator!" Lulu yelped sternly.

"Yeah, scram!" King called out. "This pool's for people and sometimes dogs!"

"Stop scaring these kids!" Hugo barked. "Or else!"

The alligator didn't move. It just kept floating there, with that annoying smirk on its face. The dogs gave one another a look. If they wanted to protect these kids, they were going to have to use force.

King jumped on the gator first, then Hugo, then Lulu, then Napoleon. They clawed at it with their paws until—*POP!*

"Uh-oh. What was that sound?" Hugo asked.

The *pop* sound was sudden and short, but followed by a long, slow *HISS*. The dogs shared looks of confusion as the alligator started to shrink underneath them. Pretty soon, they were standing in the water of the shallow end, on top of a wrinkled, flattened alligator.

One of the children began whining again. "Oh nooooo . . ."

"Guys . . . ," Lulu said. "I'm starting to think this wasn't a real alligator."

"It was a balloon! A toy," Hugo said, realizing they'd just made a giant mistake.

"A *toy*?" King said excitedly. "I LOVE toys!!! Maybe these humans DID know I was coming!" He wagged his tail as he dug into what was left of the alligator with his paws and teeth. Napoleon joined in.

"King, buddy, not all toys are for dogs—" Hugo started, trying to stop his friend from tearing up the alligator. But he was too late. The whole thing was already in shreds. Hugo watched with dismay as the torn gator pieces floated away to different parts of the pool.

Kids were screaming and pointing at the torn-up alligator and at Hugo, Lulu, King, and Napoleon. Everyone was staring at them. Most of the kids were huddled on the deck, watching them with sad, suspicious eyes. If the adults had looked mad before, they were even madder now. And the kids were definitely afraid. Not of the alligator. Of the dogs.

No way, thought Hugo. *I'm not a scary dog! Kids love me! I'm such a good dog . . . or at least . . . I was . . .*

Some of the counselors were frantically trying to clean up the mess. Hugo could hear some others talking loudly into their phones.

"They just came in and starting running around! We don't know what to do."

"None of them are wearing collars. Must be strays."

"They might be dangerous! I mean, who knows if they've had their shots?"

"Yeah, it's a golden retriever, and a bulldog, and that one might be a collie . . . and a terrier. Actually, that one kind of looks like a dog I follow on Instagram."

"We have no more lunch left for the kids! They ruined it!"

Scanning the expressions on the faces of the humans around the pool, Hugo couldn't help but feel like he'd seen these looks before. These were the same expressions that had been on the faces of the bakers in the pastry shop. The boy whose ice cream they'd stolen. Erin, after Napoleon had stolen her scarf yesterday. And all those people who had surrounded Napoleon after he'd run off into the fountain. They looked so upset, like Mom used to look when Hugo pooped on the kitchen floor. He hadn't done that since he was a puppy, since he'd learned that for some reason, humans don't like poop on their floors.

He started to realize something. *People don't always like it when dogs act funny and wild,* Hugo thought. Some of them might be amused and entertained for a little bit, and that attention felt great. But just because you made some people laugh, it didn't mean others weren't getting angry. And it was definitely possible to go too far. Like stealing their lunch or breaking their big weird toy, Hugo realized.

Humans, Hugo thought. *I love you, you complicated creatures.*

Hugo started to feel embarrassed. Sure, he'd had a great time at the pool and eaten some really delicious barbecue potato chips . . . but at what cost? He was having a great day, but had he ruined the days of all these people? Had he made kids upset?

"Time to go!" Napoleon announced as he walked back onto the dry pavement of the deck. "But first, I'm grabbing another sandwich."

Napoleon stopped by the toppled-over snack table, but Hugo had no appetite. He looked around at the trouble and destruction they had caused, and he felt terrible. What he longed for more than anything else was to be back at home, on his favorite part of the couch, watching his family watch their shiny, flickering, funny rectangle. Even if they had gotten too busy for him, he still loved

them, and they loved him. And he felt comfortable there.

"Napoleon's right," Lulu said. "We should get out of here. I think that teenaged human recognizes me from the internet. What if Jasmine finds out I was here?"

The angry voices around the pool were growing louder. And then Hugo heard one in particular that made his ears perk up.

"That one looks like Hugo!" a little girl shouted from across the pool. Hugo recognized it immediately—he would know that voice anywhere.

Zoe.

He shook some wet hair out of his eyes and turned to look. It *was* Zoe.

"But it can't be Hugo," Zoe said to her friend. "Hugo's a *good* dog! He would never do something like this."

Hugo stared at her, stunned. He suddenly felt like his favorite ball in the world had just rolled off a cliff.

King gave him a nudge. "You okay? Me and Lulu are getting out of here. Let's go!"

Hugo didn't answer.

"Hugo?" King said urgently. "Come on!"

"Let's go before I get recognized again!" Lulu added. "My followers would *not* be cool with this behavior."

Hugo snapped out of it and followed Lulu and King out of the water. They ran across the deck and out to the sidewalk. But Zoe's words kept ringing in Hugo's head.

Hugo's a good *dog. He would never . . .*

He would never . . .

CHAPTER 10

KING FELT ALIVE! He huddled with Lulu and Hugo behind some bushes next to the pool parking lot, far away from the entrance, so that no one would spot them. Napoleon was still inside the pool area, causing who knew what kind of trouble.

"That was wild," King said, out of breath. "I've never been in a pool before. There's so much water in there! Is that what all pools are like? Do all pools have snacks? If so, pools are my favorite thing in the world."

Then he remembered the looks on everyone's faces after the dogs ate all the snacks and tore up the pool toy. He could tell that Lulu and Hugo were thinking the same thing.

"At least we had fun, right?" King tried to look on the bright side.

"Right . . . ," said Lulu, but King could tell she didn't mean it.

The more King's nerves calmed down, the more his excitement was turning into regret. Jumping into the pool *had* been fun, but it definitely didn't feel good, making those kids and counselors angry. King wanted people to like him! Being a real dog could be fun, but maybe it wasn't as fun as being good and making people happy.

Hugo looked at Lulu and King. "You two are freaked out, huh?"

"Maybe a little," King admitted. "How can you tell?"

"I can see it in your eyes," Hugo replied. "You feel the same way I do. I just can't stop thinking about what Zoe said when she saw me. 'Hugo's a *good* dog. He would never do something like this.' I let her down." Hugo hung his head.

King wished he could make Hugo feel better. He looked so sad.

"Actually," Hugo said, "I think I'm done with this. Sure, being a *real* dog was fun for a bit, but now I don't even recognize myself. Maybe I'm not meant to be a real dog. Just a *good* dog."

King couldn't help but agree. "Same," he said. "I know I can get a little wild sometimes, but I don't think I liked how that felt. I have a bad feeling in my tummy. Because of what we did, but also because I ate way too much. I think I need Erin to tell me when to stop being wild. And when to stop eating. Let's just say . . . you shouldn't stand too close to me."

"I'm with you guys," Lulu added. "It was fun at first, but now it feels kind of tired. Like rhinestone collars. And besides, what is a real dog anyway, huh?! Just because I wear leather vests and tiny, bedazzled hats, am I any less of a dog? No! Plus, I don't want my Insta followers to get the wrong idea. A lot of people look up to me, you know. Well, they look down to me, since I'm a dog, but you get it . . ."

Hugo glanced at the sky. "The sun is low," he said thoughtfully. "That means camp is almost over. And after the kids come home, then . . ."

"The adults," King concluded.

"Exactly."

Right at that moment, Napoleon came running out of the gate, happy as ever.

"How amazing was *that*?!" he said, totally missing the somber mood of the group. "Man oh man, it's been *weeks* since I've been in a pool. That was awesome. And those sandwiches, what was that?! Some kind of turkey with a pesto aioli? My taste buds were doing somersaults. What a treat. Definitely one of the top ten sandwiches I've eaten today. Anyway, what's next? Should we dig up a garden? Run through a grocery store? Eat a block of cheese and barf on a rug?"

King didn't want to do any of those things. But Napoleon was so excited, King didn't know how he could ever let him down.

Hugo bravely stepped up to the plate instead. "Sorry, Napoleon. But we've actually decided to go home. Thanks for showing us a good time today, but our humans are going to be worried about us."

For a moment, Napoleon looked disappointed.

Wow, thought King, *he really likes us. I should go give him a lick on his face to show I care.*

But then Napoleon's face changed, and King suddenly realized he wasn't sad—he was *mad*. Furious, even!

"I thought you all wanted to be *real* dogs," Napoleon growled. Lulu, Hugo, and King all took a step back.

"We thought so too," said Hugo, trying not to make Napoleon angrier. "But it just doesn't feel right. We don't feel like ourselves."

"Why's that?" snapped Napoleon. "Because you don't want to disappoint your precious humans? What have they *ever* done for you? A whole lot of nothing, that's what!"

"That's not true!" said Hugo. "Sometimes when my family makes dinner, they cut up a piece of chicken just for me and mix it into my dog food!"

"And Jasmine lets me sleep on her head at night," said Lulu. "And she takes me with her everywhere, and she spends all her time making me look nice and feel nice, and she tells me all the time that I'm her best friend!"

"And Erin found me at the dog shelter and took me home to a nice house where I have lots of toys to play with!" said King. "And she didn't even get mad at me when I got sick from eating too much grass!"

"Oh yeah?" Napoleon retorted. "And you think they'll keep doing nice things for you, after everything you've done today?"

King thought about it. Maybe Napoleon had a point. He'd been really bad today. What would Erin think? "If Erin found out about her scarf, she'd probably never forgive me," he said.

Lulu felt her fur with a paw. Her blowout had turned into a giant curly, frizzy mess. "I do wonder if Jasmine will still want to be BFFs once she's seen what I've done to her beautiful blowout."

"And my family already has less time for me," added Hugo. "Once they see I destroyed the *thing*, they'll probably never want to see me again."

Napoleon's mood was suddenly brighter. "You see, pals?" he said. "There's no reason to rush home. You'll just be punished when you get there, so why don't you live it up now?"

"I don't know . . . ," said Hugo, but Napoleon wasn't going to let it go.

"Look over there," Napoleon said. He was looking across the street, into the backyard of a nearby house, where King could see a lot of children jumping up and down on a big colorful bouncy castle. "A kid's birthday party. Jackpot! This is every dog's dream."

"Not mine. I only ever have dreams where I'm running," said King. "But I'm upset about it for some reason."

Hugo and Lulu shared a wary look. King felt the same way.

"Look," said Napoleon. "Why don't you all just wait outside the backyard gate. I'll go get one more sandwich, bounce a bit, leave a little present for the birthday girl, by which I mean a poop on the grass, and then we'll all go home!"

The Good Dogs thought about this idea. It didn't seem so bad. They wouldn't have to do anything. And it would all be over soon either way.

"Fine, we'll wait out there for you. But that's it!" Lulu said firmly. "Make it quick."

"Fine," said Napoleon.

With that he darted off, and the other dogs walked slowly and carefully across the street to wait by their meeting spot. They watched as Napoleon walked confidently into the party through the open gate and grabbed a sandwich off the table.

How many sandwiches has this guy eaten today? King wondered.

But then, instead of coming right back, Napoleon went totally wild! He gulped down the sandwich, then grabbed a bunch of cupcakes and ate those too! He jumped onto a pile of gifts and started tearing up all the gift wrap and bows. Parents chased him around the yard, but no one could catch him. As he leapt onto the bouncy castle, a bunch of kids ran out of it screaming and crying. King knew that look—they were scared of Napoleon.

One little girl ran all the way out of the party toward the bushes.

"I know what to do," Hugo said. "I'll make her feel better."

Hugo went up to her and softly nudged her hand with his snout. He tried to give a gentle lick, but as soon as she saw him, she screamed and ran away from him too.

Oh no, King thought. *This is terrible.* Dogs were supposed to make children feel happy! But now, because of Napoleon, all these children were sad.

King felt worse than he'd ever felt in his life. Even worse than when he'd eaten all that grass and his stomach wouldn't stop doing flips. He realized that Erin must have felt the same way when she first met Napoleon. He had spent all day thinking that Erin's rules were getting in the way of him having fun, when really she was just helping him, and those around him, stay safe and happy. He started to whimper. *Oh, Erin!* He missed her smile, he missed her laugh, he missed the smell of food on her hands. But most of all, he missed the way she loved him, and encouraged him to be his best self.

Just then, they heard a loud sound! It sounded like a huge car zooming toward them from a distance. King spun around to see a big white van barreling around the corner, heading straight toward the house.

It skidded to the curb right near the dogs. The doors slammed open, and two men jumped out holding big nets. Animal control!

"Run!" Hugo shouted, and Lulu, King, and Hugo ran as fast as they could away from the scary men in gray uniforms. But the men were fast! King ran through the legs of one of them, narrowly avoiding a swinging net. Then the dogs darted behind a row of tall hedges, hiding as they watched the animal control officers run right past without spotting them. The dogs stopped to catch their breath, safe for the moment. But where were the officers going . . . ?

King turned to see the backyard birthday party in the distance. The officers were running straight for it. The bouncy castle wobbled back and forth, and King realized it was deflating.

"Oh no," gasped Lulu. "Napoleon must have popped the bouncy castle with his nails!"

Grown-ups were pulling kids out of the castle as it ran out of air. Everyone was running around screaming. Finally, King spotted Napoleon struggling to get out from under what was now a completely deflated castle.

"Come on, Napoleon!" shouted King. "You can do it!"

Lulu and Hugo barked encouragement as well.

Napoleon's head was poking out now, and it seemed he had found his means of escape. Then, seemingly from out of nowhere, King, Lulu, and Hugo watched as animal control grabbed Napoleon from under the castle and carried him to the van. The dogs carefully leaned through the hedges to get a better look. Napoleon was sitting in a metal cage in the back of the van. He looked at them sadly, then turned away. King, Hugo, and Lulu shared a worried frown. There was nothing they could do. They knew this day had gone totally off the rails, but this was worse than anything they ever could have imagined!

The officers shut the doors, then glanced around one last time.

"Hey, did you see where those other dogs went?" one of the men asked.

"No," the other man answered. "But I have a sneaking suspicion this little guy's their ringleader. If those
dogs cause any more trouble, we'll be back."

King gulped. "What do we do now?"

Lulu sniffed the air and looked disgusted. "Yuck,
King!" she said. "Was that you?"

"What?" he said. "I told you not to stand too close
to me."

CHAPTER 11

"WELL, THAT'S THAT," said Lulu, trying to sound cheerful. "Napoleon's off to the pound and King stinks. Guess we can all go home!"

Hugo and King just stared at her with their mouths agape.

"What?" asked Lulu. "Do I have, like, food on my face or something? Ew, ew, ew!"

"No," said Hugo. "It's just . . . don't you think we should help Napoleon?"

"I don't even know where the shelter is," she replied. "And look, I'm not saying that Napoleon got what was coming to him, but I bet *some* would say . . . that he got what was coming to him. Not me. I would never say that, obviously, because I'm so nice. Too nice. It's practically a flaw. But some would say it!"

"That might be true," said Hugo. "But *we* were being bad all day too. Any of us could have been taken to the shelter by animal control. It's sheer luck that we weren't."

Lulu still wasn't buying it. If there was one thing she'd learned today, it was that being bad wasn't for her. She just wanted to go home, put on a face mask, and watch a bad reality show with Jasmine on the shiny rectangle.

"But we said we wouldn't be bad anymore," she squeaked. "We knew when to call it quits. We're just good dogs having a *bad day*, like you said! We're not *bad* dogs like Napoleon. We shouldn't have to suffer because of him."

Hugo sighed a deep sigh. He was lost in thought.

King, who had been quiet for a while, suddenly piped up. "I noticed something. When we were all saying nice things about our humans, Napoleon didn't have anything to add. His boy at the park seemed really distracted the day we met him, like he barely noticed Napoleon was there. And we *never* see him at doggy day care."

"King, what're you trying to say?" asked Lulu. He was taking a long time to get to his point.

"I'm saying that . . . maybe he's just lonely."

"I think King is right," Hugo said, looking like something had finally clicked in his head. "I know the feeling. I should have recognized it."

Lulu thought about it. She had spent so much time

being mad at Jasmine for bailing on their plans that morning that she hadn't stopped to appreciate how good she had it. The only reason she was upset about Jasmine's audition was that she was used to Jasmine fawning over her every second of every day. She was a very lucky dog. Not every dog was so lucky. Maybe Napoleon wasn't such a *bad* dog after all. Maybe he was a *good* dog who needed to be loved. Lulu had had one bad day, but perhaps Napoleon had bad days all the time . . .

"Hmm. I wonder if Napoleon just needs some attention," Lulu said. She knew how important attention could be. There was *nothing in the world* more exciting than getting attention! She suddenly felt really sorry for Napoleon. Lulu thought that a dog without attention was like an Instagram account without followers . . . beautiful but sad.

"We have to go save him," said King. "We can't leave him in the shelter. The people who work there are nice, and they try very hard to take you for walks and give you love, but nothing compares to having a family. Plus, Finn might not be the best owner, but I bet he'll miss Napoleon a lot when he realizes he's missing. We have to save him. We have to!"

Hugo and Lulu were quiet for a moment as they thought it over. Saving Napoleon was going to be hard work. And Lulu was sure they were all pretty tired after the day they had had.

♥. *Lulu*

But Hugo spoke up first. "King is right," he said. "Let's go."

So the three dogs set off in the direction the van had gone, staying close to the bushes next to the sidewalk so they'd be harder to spot. But the van was long gone now, and they had nothing to follow.

"We still don't know where the shelter is," Lulu pointed out. "How are we going to find it?"

"I used to live there," King said. "And I remember how it smelled. It smelled like . . . lots of dogs! If we can just get closer, I'll recognize it."

They kept running until they came to a fork in the road. They didn't know which way to turn. All three dogs sniffed around for clues unsuccessfully until Hugo started barking excitedly.

"Look, you guys! It's Patches!"

Sure enough, Patches was sitting at an outdoor café across the street with his owner, who was just as old as Patches, but in human years. She didn't notice at all as Lulu, King, and Hugo barked at Patches from across the road.

"Patches! Hi!" Hugo shouted. "Did you see an animal control van drive by a little while ago?"

"Which way did it go?" barked Lulu frantically.

Patches stared at them and took a deep breath. "Well . . . ," he started, "I saw a different van about five or six years back. Nice van, although what do I know about vans? I barked at it because, if you can believe it, that nice van had a rabbit peeping out the window. The rabbit looked at me and—"

"Patches, there's no time," yelped King. "Did you see an animal control van or not?"

Wow, thought Lulu, *King means business! I bet he'd be really good on Insta as a dog who dresses up in business clothes.*

"Sorry," said Patches slowly. "You mean that animal control van that passed by a few minutes ago and turned right? Yeah, I was sitting here, chewing on a stick, which reminds me of the time . . ."

But Lulu didn't hear what time that reminded Patches of, because as soon as he said that the van had turned right, she, Hugo, and King took off in that direction.

They ran down the street as fast as they could, occasionally stopping to bark for directions from other dogs downtown. A poodle tied up outside a barbershop, a shih tzu on a bench, two German shepherds on a front stoop. A lot of very observant dogs had noticed the van and were willing to help!

Before they knew it, Lulu, King, and Hugo were all the way on the other side of town. They could tell they were getting closer to the shelter, because King picked up its scent and started sniffing all around, more and more quickly. It was hard to keep up with him! Finally, they turned a corner and there it was—the animal control van!

BARK!

BARK!

"There it is!" Lulu barked. "Nice job, King!"

They kept their distance, trying not to be spotted as they followed the van down a series of side streets. Soon, the shelter came into sight. They had arrived.

"Hide!" King shouted, and they all scrambled behind some bushes.

They watched as the animal control officers parked in a small fenced area near the back door of the animal shelter.

"That's him!" King said as one officer took a medium-sized crate out of the back of the van. Then he took out two smaller crates and placed all three in the holding area.

The officer got back into the van and drove around toward the front of the building.

"Okay, this is our moment," Lulu said. "We just need to break Napoleon free before the officers come back."

"I have an idea," said King. "I can distract them using all the agility skills I've been learning! Then you two can break Napoleon out from his crate."

"Perfect!" said Hugo.

One of the officers was now walking back toward the holding area. The time was *now*.

King turned to them. "When Erin wants to distract me, she throws a squeaky ball and I run after it," he said. "Today . . . I *am* the squeaky ball."

Then he leapt out from behind the bushes and

started pulling out all the stops to distract the officer. He leapt over a nearby fence. He danced on his hind legs. He wiggled and jumped. He ran in circles, and in and out between the officer's legs. He did somersaults! It was incredible. If Lulu kept watching, even *she'd* get distracted.

Under different circumstances, thought Lulu, *I'd be nudging Jasmine to get her camera out.*

But there was no time to build a social media strategy around King at this moment. They had to act fast! King ran along the side of the building, getting the officer to chase him away from the back. With the coast clear, Lulu and Hugo ran over to the holding area and saw what they were working with.

"I don't think we can get over the fence," said Lulu. "It's too high!"

"There has to be a way," said Hugo, and he turned to Napoleon. "We're going to get you out!"

"Oh, don't bother," said Napoleon quietly from his crate on the other side of the fence. "Just go on with your lives; I'm a goner. I have no one to blame but myself."

Napoleon took a deep, sad breath, then continued. "It's just . . . well, Finn never really paid much attention to me, so I guess it felt good to have friends. Even if it was just for the day. But I took it too far. I took it all too far. I really am a bad dog. I deserve whatever I get."

"Oh, come on," Hugo said, trying to cheer Napoleon up. "You're not a bad dog. You're . . . you're only . . ." Hugo trailed off, and a look of understanding spread across his face. "You know what? I just realized something." Hugo turned from Napoleon to Lulu, then back to Napoleon. "There's no such thing as good dogs and bad dogs. We're all just *dogs* making decisions every day. Sometimes we make good decisions, and sometimes we make bad ones. Maybe today you made more bad decisions than good ones, but you still deserve a second chance. And there will always be tomorrow. We're all just trying to do our best."

"Wow," said Napoleon, lifting his head from his paws. "That's the most beautiful thing I've ever heard. And I've heard bacon sizzling."

Lulu knew right away that Hugo was right. And that she had to help Napoleon.

She'd spent the whole day trying to act like a "real dog," and she had realized something similar to Hugo. There's no one way to be a real dog. A real dog can eat fancy breakfasts *and* dirty hot dogs. A real dog can dress up in stylish outfits for Instagram *and* run fully nude through a fountain. A real dog can have wild adventures *and* stay at home and relax with her people. Maybe she and her friends had always been real dogs, from the beginning.

Well, Lulu thought, *this real dog helps her friends.*

"It's true!" she said. "Now, if I could just get over this fence, I bet I could unlock your crate. I know how to unlock mine!"

"I can help! I can help!" A little voice was coming from one of the smaller crates. Lulu saw that it belonged to a tiny puppy who was so fluffy, you could have mistaken it for a cozy golden-brown pillow. "I want to help!"

Lulu wasn't an expert in dog breeds, but if she had to guess, she'd say this puppy was some kind of fluffo duffo. Or maybe a fluffo duffo poofy puffo mix? Whatever she was, her excited yapping was getting louder.

"Shh!" Lulu said to the puppy. "Quiet! You might draw attention to us!"

"Let me help! Let me help! I want to help! I'm a good helper!" the puppy kept barking.

"Well, hello there," said Hugo gently, and she somehow calmed down immediately to listen. The tone of his bark was soothing and kind. He was clearly very good with puppies. "Where did you come from?"

"I was picked up by the school today," the puppy responded.

"Okay," Hugo said patiently. "Where's your family?"

"Me and my mom and all my siblings were strays,"

the puppy explained. "They were all picked up by animal control last week, but I just kept wandering, and now I think I might be very far from where I was born . . ."

"Don't worry," said Lulu. "If you help us, we'll break you out too."

Hugo turned to Lulu and lowered his voice so that the puppy couldn't hear. "And do what with her?"

"We will fetch that stick when we get to it," replied Lulu through her teeth. "We have bigger things to worry about. Like how I'm going to get over this fence."

"I think I have an idea," said Hugo with a smile. "What if we didn't go over the fence? What if we went *under* the fence? We could dig a hole!"

"Genius!" said Lulu, wagging her tail. "Good thing we got so much practice digging holes today."

With that, they both went to work.

"It's fun using our bad-dog skills for good," Hugo said.

"Yeah! We're being really good bad dogs," Lulu replied as she tore at the mud with all her paws.

"Use your whole body! Not just your paws," shouted Napoleon, and they both dug even harder. "Yeah, just like that! Make sure you dig the hole really, really big. Bigger than it needs to be. That's Hole Digging 101!"

They kept digging until the hole was huge. Lulu was getting dirt all over her beautiful fur, but she didn't even care. She was on a mission! Soon she could crawl inside the hole and under the fence. When she got to the other side, she ran and unlocked the puppy's crate easily. Then she rushed over to Napoleon's crate and attempted to get it open, but it wouldn't budge. She tried again. Still no luck.

"I don't know how this one works," she said, exasperated. "The lock is different from mine at home. Ugh! If only I had smaller paws, like . . ."

"Like mine?" asked a voice from the other small crate, and a tiny feline paw appeared between the bars.

The voice sounded very familiar. Lulu got closer to the crate. "Pickle?!" she asked, shocked.

"You finally used your little brain and figured it out," said Pickle, cruel as ever. "After you savagely trapped me outside my yard, I wandered downtown, where I attracted lots of attention by attacking a balloon outside a delicious-smelling bakery. Soon, I was surrounded by admirers. Unfortunately, two of those admirers turned out to be animal control officers, who shoved me into a cage in a van and brought me *here*. Those *dogs* at animal control put me in here with a bunch of *dogs*. They're a bunch of *bathtubs*, if you ask me."

"Pickle, this is great news," said Lulu.

"Is it?" asked Pickle. "Because from where I'm standing, it feels like bad news."

"Well, see, the crate you're in *is* the same as mine,"

explained Lulu. "The lock is the same. So I can let you out. But you have to *promise* that you'll let Napoleon out afterward and not just run away."

"Oh, I don't know," said Pickle, looking over at Napoleon's crate. "I seem to recall that last time I was in trouble, it was because a certain *dog* bumped me out of my tree."

"Well, I'm sorry we got you stranded outside of your yard," Lulu said. "We only did it because you're always so mean to us."

"What do you care? You have each other to keep you busy. And all those other dogs at Erin's house. All I have is my tree and brilliant zingers. So what if I make fun of you? It's how I pass the time—plus, I'm hilarious."

So Pickle is lonely, Lulu thought. *Just like Napoleon. Just like everybody sometimes.* That's why she was always mean to them. She was lonely, and probably even a little jealous. It was true that they had one another. Maybe she just needed a friend!

"You're right, Pickle," said Lulu.

Pickle perked up. "I am?" She purred. "Of course I am. I love to be right."

"You're right about a lot of stuff," Lulu added. "Like... we *are* slobbery! And we're loud! There's sooo much we could learn from you. Maybe when we all get outta here, you could teach us how to be cleaner and ... and ..."

"More lovable?" asked Pickle.

"Yeah," said Lulu. "Sure! More lovable!"

"Hmm," said Pickle, thinking out loud. "It would be a lot of work. And I don't know if I could ever make you less slobbery—I'm a cat, not a magician—but we could try."

Lulu wagged her tail. Hugo did too. This was progress!

"And maybe I could dig a secret hole under your fence so that if you ever get locked out, there's a way back in," offered Hugo.

Pickle thought for what felt like a century. "Okay," she finally said. "I'll help your friend."

The dogs all cheered as Lulu unlocked Pickle's crate. Pickle then made quick work of opening Napoleon's crate—she really was nimble—and within seconds, he was free too. Then Lulu, Napoleon, Pickle,

and the puppy ran out through the hole, joining Hugo on the other side of the fence.

That's when they heard the voice.

"Stop those dogs!"

It was the animal control officer running back around the building. Uh-oh!

CHAPTER 12

T HE DOGS, ALONG with their puppy and cat accomplices, ran as fast as they could away from the shelter as the officer quickly hopped into his van. Hugo turned to see King catching up with them.

"Sorry I let that officer get away!" King said, panting as he ran his fastest.

"That's okay," Lulu said. "You couldn't distract him forever. You were a wonderful squeaky ball!"

They shot out of the shelter's parking lot, but the van was gaining on them.

"What do we do?" asked King nervously as the van got closer and closer. "If he catches us . . ." King trailed off, shuddering.

"Let's split up!" said Hugo, thinking fast. "He can't chase all of us at once. We'll meet up at the dumpster where we left our collars."

"Good idea," said Napoleon. "Pickle, it's just behind the bakery with the balloons. Where you—ah—were surrounded by admirers."

Lulu and King nodded in agreement.

"Sure, I suppose that's worth a try," said Pickle begrudgingly. "I wouldn't mind seeing some of my fans again."

"But . . . ," the puppy whined softly. "I don't know where that is. Or how to get there. I'm not even really sure what a dumpster is!"

"Whoa, cool! A puppy who's even younger than me," King interjected.

"Stick with me," Hugo said to the puppy. And as soon as they got to the next intersection, all the dogs and Pickle scattered, running wildly in different directions.

The van skidded to a halt, and turning to look over his shoulder, Hugo could see a confused expression on the officer's face. It was the same as the look on Mom's face when the kids were all running around too fast for her to keep up. The only difference was that Mom's expression was still full of love.

It was every dog or cat for themselves now, except for Hugo, who made sure the puppy kept up. They bolted through the busy downtown streets, doing their best to outrun and evade the van.

"This way!" Hugo called. Then, "That way! Quick!" As they crossed a street, a van stopped in front of them, blocking their path. *Uh-oh*, Hugo thought. But then he looked up to see that it was a different van! *Phew*.

"For a second, I thought it was the animal control officer," Hugo said.

"Um . . . ," the puppy replied, turning to look behind them. Hugo turned, and barked in shock. The officer's van was coming right at them from the other direction!

"Gotcha," the officer said. Or at least that's what it looked like from far away. Hugo was pretty good at reading lips. It was either *gotcha* or *goat cheese*, but Hugo figured that *gotcha* made a lot more sense in this context.

"I think we're stuck," said the puppy.

"Follow me," Hugo said confidently. Then he crouched and ran quickly underneath the van in front of them. Once they were through, they sprinted down the sidewalk.

"Don't worry, we're close to the dumpster," Hugo said. "I think it's just around here—"

But before he could finish, a little boy and a little girl jumped up from their seats at an outdoor café and got in front of him.

"Mommy, look!" the little girl screamed excitedly. "Two doggies! Can we pet them?"

"Please, Mommy? Can we, please?" the boy added.

"Can we let them pet us, Hugo?" the puppy asked, giving Hugo some sweet, pleading puppy-dog eyes. "Pleeeaaaase."

Hugo thought about it. One quick pet couldn't hurt, he decided.

"All right, but then we have to run!" Hugo said, stopping and sitting for a moment as the kids' hands ran through his fur. He kept his eyes on the street behind them, in case the van turned the corner.

The pets, pats, and rubs were wonderful. But Hugo knew the dumpster was nearby, and that they needed to get there as soon as possible.

Just then, a voice Hugo knew shouted from across the street.

"I recognize that dog!"

It was the baker from the café.

"That's one of those dogs who messed up my kitchen! Someone catch it!"

And then the officer's van turned the corner!

"Well," Hugo said, turning to the puppy. "Now it's *really* time to run. Come on, before he sees us!"

They bolted as fast as they could, under the legs of the kids and through a lot of tables and chairs at the outdoor café until they reached the end of the block. They turned the corner onto a smaller street, still running their fastest until Hugo stopped abruptly. He held his nose in the air, sniffing his surroundings, and then found it.

"There!" Hugo said, nodding to a nearby alleyway. He led the puppy down the alley until they reached the dumpster. Pickle was waiting for them.

"Did I mention that cats are *faster* than dogs?" Pickle asked.

"I'm not sure," Hugo answered, out of breath.

"Well, I did!" Pickle said proudly. "Of course you don't remember. Cats also have better memories than dogs, and—"

Pickle was interrupted by the puppy's yelps. She was barking at the sight of Lulu running down the alley toward them.

"Shh," Hugo said to the puppy. "We don't want the officer to hear us."

When Lulu got to the dumpster, she was relieved to see that Hugo and the puppy were already there. "Sorry that took me so long," she said. "I stopped to get some pets."

"Oh, so did we!" said the puppy.

Pretty soon after that, King arrived, wagging his tail with delight as he saw that Hugo and Lulu were safe and sound.

"Whew! That was close," King said, sniffing his friends' butts. "He almost caught me . . . and then I stopped for a minute to get some pets."

"Did we all stop for pets?" Hugo asked.

"I didn't," came Napoleon's voice as he trotted down the alley toward the dumpster. He had a long stick of salami hanging out of his mouth. "I stopped for a snack."

They each found their collars behind the dumpster and helped one another wiggle them back on.

"Hello, King," King greeted himself as Lulu helped him slip his collar over his neck. "It's good to see you again."

"We should split up and go home," Hugo pointed out. "We don't have much time. The officer could catch up to us soon."

"My house is close to here," Pickle said. Then she lowered her voice and looked away. "But I might need . . . a little . . . um . . ." Pickle lowered her voice even more, embarrassed. "A little . . . *help* . . . getting back into my yard."

Hugo, Lulu, and King shared a look.

"Can you say that a little louder?" Lulu asked. "You, a cat, need help from us, 'dirty,' 'stinky' *dogs*?"

Pickle huffed and then led all the dogs out of the alley.

They carefully looked both ways to make sure the officer wasn't in sight, then cautiously followed Pickle back to her house. Walking through the tree-lined streets, Hugo took in the familiar scent of the grass of his neighborhood. He recognized the bushes and the dirt, and he was pretty sure he could smell King's pee, from before.

"Ah, the sweet, sweet smell of my own pee," King said, also noticing. "We're almost home!"

When they got to Pickle's house, her front door was locked, and the gate to the backyard was still closed.

"If I could just get a boost, I could jump back into my tree," Pickle said. "Then I can get over the fence and into the yard."

Hugo was the tallest of all the dogs, so they immediately turned to him. Helping Pickle wasn't something he was super excited to do, after the way she had treated them . . . but then he remembered that he was part of the reason she was locked out of her yard in the first place. Plus, helping someone in need is what a good dog would do, he thought.

"All right, get on my back," Hugo said. "But be carefu—OWW!"

Pickle, sprightly as ever, was already on his back, and boy, did her claws hurt. Hugo stood up as tall as he could and positioned himself underneath the tree.

"Okay, ready to jump?" Hugo asked.

"I was born ready to jump," Pickle replied confidently. "Every cat is."

"All right. One, two . . ." But before Hugo could get to three, Pickle had jumped off his back, high into the air, and landed successfully on her branch. Hugo immediately felt relieved that her sharp claws were out of his fur.

Pickle turned away and spoke softly again. "Uh . . . I want to say . . . like . . . thank you . . . or whatever."

"What was that, Pickle?" Lulu asked, turning her ear closer to the tree. "We really can't hear you when you whisper."

"I said . . . THANK YOU!" Pickle turned to face them. "I appreciate the help."

"You're welcome!" said King.

"I promise to be sort of . . . a little bit . . . nicer to you. In the future," Pickle said. And then Hugo was pretty sure he heard her mutter, "For a week or so, anyway . . ." as she jumped out of the tree and into her backyard, out of sight.

"My place is a few blocks away," Napoleon said. "I'll get going now. See you guys around, I guess."

Napoleon started to walk off alone, but King barked to get his attention. "Hey!" he called out. "We'll come with you. In case you need any help sneaking back in."

"I should be all right on my own," Napoleon said, but King, Lulu, and Hugo followed behind, with the puppy still sticking close to Hugo's side.

"We insist!" said Lulu.

"We've been following you around all day," Hugo said. "What's one more stop?"

Hugo assumed it would be easy to sneak Napoleon back into his house. After all, Finn seemed to pay very little attention to Napoleon's comings and goings.

When they got to the house, King wagged his tail. "This is where you live? I've definitely peed on this lawn."

"So have I," Lulu said, sniffing the grass.

"Same," Hugo chimed in. This was a solid lawn for doing his business, both kinds. He'd smelled the scent of dog on the grass, but hadn't realized that one actually lived here. He had just thought it was a popular place for the pee-ers and poopers of the neighborhood. "How come we've never seen you before yesterday in the park?"

"Haven't been here long," Napoleon said. "Just moved in a couple months ago, and my people have been a bit busy adjusting to new jobs and new friends and stuff."

They were surprised to see the front door propped open. It looked like they wouldn't have to do much sneaking after all, Hugo thought. Napoleon turned to the other dogs when they reached the edge of the lawn.

"Today was pretty fun," Napoleon said softly, with an expression on his face that Hugo hadn't seen before. "I'm sorry if I ever went too far. Can't help it sometimes."

"That's okay," Hugo said with a smile. "We've all been there."

"Yeah," Lulu agreed. "It was nice getting to know another dog in the neighborhood!"

Hugo, Lulu, and King affectionately sniffed Napoleon's butt goodbye, then hid in the bushes to watch as Napoleon slowly trotted up the front path toward his house. Before he could reach the front door, two adult humans burst through it, running out onto the lawn to embrace him.

The dogs all watched, surprised, as the two adults fawned all over Napoleon, giving him millions of pets and kisses.

"This must be the wrong house," King said. "These people look like they *like* him."

"I think those are his people parents!" Hugo said, watching the curious scene unfold.

"Napoleon!!! Oh my gosh, you're okay!" Napoleon's dad said.

"Where were you, little guy? We were so worried!" His mom gave him a huge hug as Finn, the teenager from the park, walked out onto the front stoop. Hugo was pretty good at sensing human emotions, and although he could tell Finn was happy to see Napoleon, he was also something else: embarrassed.

"When animal control called and said they had him, but he escaped . . . I wasn't sure he'd make it back here." Napoleon's dad scratched him behind his ears.

"We were so worried," Napoleon's mom said again. "Thank goodness for your microchip! But you better not wander off again, okay?"

They turned back toward the house and spotted Finn standing there, by the doorway.

"You're in big trouble, kiddo," Napoleon's dad said to Finn. "You can't let him sneak out like that."

Finn mumbled something, then dropped to his knees and gave Napoleon some hugs too.

"You're grounded until you prove you can take better care of him," the dad said sternly, and Finn nodded apologetically.

"And I still think we should talk about some basic training classes," the mom said. Hugo could see what looked like a mixture of excitement and horror on Napoleon's face.

"You're right," the dad added. "We were so busy with the move, we didn't have time. But it's a good idea."

"That nice woman Erin, from the neighborhood association, gave us some recommendations."

"That's great! I'll make some calls," Napoleon's dad said. Then he looked back down to Napoleon. "How'd you get back home, anyway?"

Napoleon glanced into the bushes. Hugo, Lulu, King, and the puppy scattered quickly into entirely different bushes to avoid being seen by the humans. The dad followed Napoleon's gaze into the distance. Hugo couldn't be sure whether they had been spotted.

"I guess you must have some friends in the neighborhood," Napoleon's dad said as they walked inside together. Hugo thought he saw Napoleon's tail wag upon hearing that.

Napoleon gave them one last glance over his shoulder as the door closed behind him, and his new friends all wagged their tails goodbye.

LULU THOUGHT ABOUT how she would fix her fur as they made their way back to her house. She'd have to move quickly to restore her perfect floofiness before Jasmine got home so that Jasmine wouldn't notice anything odd.

She knew where Jasmine kept the doggy hair products. Maybe she could get into that drawer, twist off the caps with her teeth, and rub some through her fur? The groomer usually used a blow-dryer, which might be hard to operate by herself. But maybe if Hugo and King helped her sneak back inside, and one of them held the blow-dryer while the other pressed the button . . . The only thing she knew for sure was that she couldn't let Jasmine see her like *this*.

"Lulu! *There* you are!"

Lulu turned to see Jasmine holding the door open. Lulu quickly forgot all about trying to sneak in or fix her appearance. Her tail started wagging wildly upon seeing her best friend.

"Where have you been?!" Jasmine asked. "Oh my gosh, you're a mess! When I got home and you weren't here, I was so worried. Don't you ever do that again!"

Jasmine noticed the other dogs, and puppy, standing in the driveway.

"And Hugo and King? What are you guys doing here? And a little fluffo duffo? I don't recognize you . . ."

Lulu gave the other dogs a quick nod goodbye, then ran up the lawn, through the doorway, and into

Jasmine's arms. As Jasmine lifted her up, Lulu whipped out her tongue and licked every last part of her best friend's face. Then she licked it all again.

I've tasted a lot of delicious things today, Lulu thought. *But Jasmine's face is still the best of the best.*

"Wow, girl," Jasmine laughed as she closed the door and brought Lulu into the kitchen. "It's okay, I'm not mad! I'm just so glad you found your way home. It makes my day even better!"

Even better? Lulu wondered.

"I got the part!" Jasmine exclaimed. "I'm going to be in a MOVIE!"

Lulu jumped up and down excitedly.

"I've been so excited to tell you all day," Jasmine said. "Oh, and don't worry! I already talked to the producers. They're cool with me bringing you to the set every day."

Lulu wagged her tail at the thought. She was about to be a *movie star*. Or, even better: a *movie star's dog*! But then she had another thought. Would this mean she wouldn't get to see Hugo and King anymore? They'd had so much fun today . . .

As if reading Lulu's mind, Jasmine continued. "Or maybe not every day. You might like to spend some time at Good Dogs too," she said, looking over Lulu's muddy fur and smiling. "It must be fun getting to be a dog sometimes, huh?"

Jasmine prepared the table for a celebratory meal, and Lulu noticed a white paper bag on the counter that she recognized. She whimpered at it and nudged it with her paw.

"Oh, girl, that was a surprise for dessert!" Jasmine said. "But you can have a little piece now. To celebrate!"

She opened it up to reveal two delicious-looking and, more important, delicious-smelling vanilla cupcakes.

"They're from the Chic Patisserie," Jasmine said.

Lulu laughed to herself. She'd have to tell Hugo and King about this the next time she saw them. At first she wasn't sure if she could eat another cupcake—she'd already eaten more baked goods in one day than she had in the past month! But who was she kidding? She scarfed it down enthusiastically and licked Jasmine's hands to say thank you.

As Lulu settled into her cozy throne at the table, across from Jasmine, and started slowly and politely eating her home-cooked meal, she couldn't help but think . . .

Jasmine's right. It is fun to act like a dog sometimes.

Lulu panted happily as Jasmine tickled her favorite spot, under the chin.

But it's also nice to come home.

KING WAS NERVOUS to go back to his house. What would Erin think? What would Cleo think?

"I guess I'll see you later," King said to Hugo, his voice shaking, as they stood in Lulu's driveway. Hugo's house was next door, and King was about to be on his own.

"I'll come with you," Hugo said. "For moral support! My house can wait."

"I'll come too! For moral support!" the puppy barked. "What's moral support?"

This cheered King up a bit, and they started walking down the street and around the corner.

When King, Hugo, and the puppy got to King's house, Erin's car was already in the driveway, which meant that she and Cleo were home. Normally, when King was inside his house, he would be thrilled when he saw Erin's car pulling into the driveway. But now he mostly felt anxious. Erin would know by now that he'd left the laundry room, and she was about to see that he'd lost his cone of shame.

Even if she never finds out about the scarf, King thought, *she'll know right away that I've been a bad dog—again.*

King took a deep breath.

"You sure you don't want us to run back to the park and grab your cone?" Hugo asked. "I'm sorry we didn't go back for it."

King shook his head. "I should just go inside. The longer I'm out, the more trouble I'll be in."

"If you're nervous, you could come home with me," Hugo offered.

"That's okay," King responded. "It's time for me to face the music. I was a bad dog. Now I have to own it. If Erin can't accept that, well ... well ..."

He thought about it for a moment, then lowered his voice. "I can't think about that right now," King said softly. "I'll just have to play it by ear. You know, lick Erin's ear a lot and see if that changes her mind."

Then the three dogs sniffed one another's butts goodbye, and King walked around the house to the back door. He climbed the two steps, took another deep breath, then gave the door a good hard scratch. He let out one of his signature whines to let them know it was him. Erin came to the door right away.

"Well, well, well . . . ," she said, shaking her head as she opened the door. "Look who came home!"

But the look on Erin's face wasn't disappointment. It was relief. He expected her to yell at him, but as soon as he walked inside, she got down on the floor, wrapped her arms around him, and gave him a ton of pets.

"Where were you?! We were all so worried, King," Erin said as Cleo also ran over and licked him affectionately.

"Finally, you're home!" Cleo said excitedly. "What happened? Are you okay???"

"Yeah, I'm okay!" King managed to say in the midst of all the hubbub.

"We were worried about you," Cleo said. "It's not like you to sneak out of the house."

"What do you mean?" King asked sheepishly. "I'm a bad dog all the time."

Cleo sighed. "You're not a *bad dog*," she said. "You just make mistakes, like we all do."

"You don't make mistakes . . . ," King said.

"Oh, I certainly do!" Cleo retorted. Then she looked away, almost as if she were embarrassed. "The reason we're home early . . . is that I totally messed up at the agility competition. I got distracted by a squirrel!"

King couldn't stop his tail from wagging.

"I mean, can you believe that?!" Cleo asked. "A squirrel! What am I, a puppy?"

King was running around now, so excited, he couldn't contain himself.

"Okay, okay, no need to gloat!" Cleo said.

"What kind of squirrel was it?" King asked. "Was it big or little? Was it fast? Did you chase it?"

"It was small and fluffy," Cleo said. "I didn't chase it, but I really wanted to!"

Then they both started laughing and laughing, and Erin picked King up to take him over to the kitchen sink.

"I wonder what happened to your cone," Erin said as she cleaned off his paw and wrapped a brand-new bandage around his cut. "I guess it wasn't much fun to wear it, huh? Well, let's see how you do without it."

When his paw was wrapped up nicely, Erin got out some food for both of the dogs . . . but something smelled different about their dinner.

"Is that . . . what I think it is?!" King said, sniffing the air.

"Here's some cheese!" Erin said as she carefully laid two big slices on top of their bowls—one for King and one for Cleo.

Cheese! Cheese! Cheese! Cheese! Cheese! King's mind was racing. *Do I eat the cheese first, then the rest of the food? Or the rest of the food first and save the cheese until the end? Or maybe I eat it all at the same time?*

King wanted to run and jump all around the house! But if he did that, it would be longer before he could eat his cheese. So he sat still and wagged his tail as hard as he could as Erin placed the bowl in front of him.

"I thought you two could use some cheering up," Erin said, petting them both on the head.

"But! But!" King said, turning to Cleo. "Our snacks are usually like—like . . . organic vegan quinoa and carrot cubes! I thought cheese was bad for dogs!"

"It's okay once in a while," Cleo said. "As a special treat."

King was about to dig into his delicious cheesy meal, but he paused and turned back to Cleo. "I'm glad Erin didn't punish me for sneaking out," he said. "I thought she'd be so mad . . . that she'd send me back to the shelter."

"Don't be silly," Cleo said, and then she got very serious. "Listen. Erin will never, ever send you back to the shelter. Okay? We love you, you little goofball. We're a family!"

Cleo nuzzled him with her head, and King nodded, smiling.

"Now, let's eat!" Cleo said, and she scarfed down her whole meal in three big mouthfuls.

"Wow! You were hungry, Cleo," Erin said, laughing.

King looked around at Erin and Cleo and his warm, cozy kitchen and delicious cheesy dinner, and his tail started wagging again. But not just because of the cheese. Because he knew he was home. For good.

HUGO AND THE puppy watched from the bottom of the driveway as King disappeared behind the house. Hugo hoped his friend wouldn't get into too much trouble with Erin, but there wasn't much he could do to help now. He realized it had gotten late, and it was time to make his way home.

"Well, I guess I'll be going now . . . ," the puppy said.

"Really? Where?" Hugo said, caught off guard.

"I'm not sure," the puppy answered. "I was living in a drainage ditch behind the school when they picked me up. But I've heard there's a nice abandoned shed over by the dump. It doesn't have a roof, but that means there will be plenty of rain puddles on the floor to drink out of."

"Forget it! That's no place to live," Hugo said. He didn't have to think very long to know what he needed to do. "Come on! You're coming home with me."

The puppy's eyes got wide, and her jaw dropped. She was speechless. Then she just repeated that word, *home*, a few times softly to herself.

"H-h-home? Home. Home?" she said. "I could have a . . . a . . . home?"

"This way!" Hugo said, leading the way home as the puppy eagerly followed. "By the way, I don't think I caught your name."

"Oh, I don't think I have one," the puppy replied. "I guess I've always thought of myself as either a Puppy, or a Lil' Puppy, or a Sweetie Puppy Girl, or something along those lines . . . But I'm open to anything."

When they got to the house, Hugo led the way through the yard to the back door. He got up on his hind legs and peeked through the window.

There they were: Hugo's family. And it looked like the usual chaos. Mom was busy on the phone, pacing back and forth while the kids were drawing at the kitchen table. Dad was running around, frantically looking for something. There were papers all over the place, and everyone was talking loudly on top of one another.

Just another weekday night at our house, Hugo thought sadly. It seemed like they hadn't even noticed he was gone. Heartbroken, he looked away from the scene and put his tail between his legs. Was it possible that they were *happy* he was gone?

As he walked through the doggy door, and the puppy followed behind him, he was suddenly able to hear the commotion inside the kitchen much more clearly.

"He's a golden retriever, about seventy pounds, twenty-three inches tall," Mom was saying into the phone. "He was here this morning. Please, please, let us know if you hear anything. Thank you."

"How's this?" Zoe asked, holding up the picture she was drawing. Hugo looked and saw that it was a picture of him! It said "Missing Dog" on it. Zoe looked like she had been crying.

"That's perfect," Sofia said, hugging her sister and adding the flyer to a pile of "Missing Dog" pictures. "I'll go put these up around the block."

"Found my keys!" Dad shouted. "Sofia, you can come with me. We'll drive around the neighborhood and look. He can't be far!"

They *had* noticed he was gone, Hugo realized. And they were more worried than he'd ever seen them. The family was so busy looking for him that they hadn't noticed him walk in, so he gave one loud bark, and everyone gasped.

Dad dropped his keys, Mom dropped the phone, and the kids all jumped up from the kitchen table. They ran as fast as they could toward Hugo and practically fell in a big pile on top of him.

"Hugo! You're back!" Enrique cried with excitement.

"Thank goodness!" Mom said, smiling as she kissed Hugo's head.

"I missed you so much!" Zoe said, giving him the biggest hug of anyone. Then she whispered in his ear, "I thought I saw you today, but it was a bad dog . . ."

Then, Zoe noticed the puppy standing sheepishly behind Hugo. And she screamed!

"OHMYGOSH OHMYGOSH! A PUPPY! A PUPPY?! A PUPPY?!!?!?"

Zoe stared at the puppy. The puppy stared at Zoe.

"YOU BROUGHT ME A PUPPY FOR MY EARLY BIRTHDAY PRESENT!" Zoe said, giving Hugo another big hug. "You always know what I want, Hugo!"

Then Zoe gave the puppy a big hug and started to cry with happiness. Hugo knew that dogs didn't cry, unless they had allergies or an underlying tear duct issue. But he could tell that if she could have, the puppy would have cried from happiness too.

As everyone crowded around Hugo and the puppy, Hugo felt a flood of relief that no one seemed mad at him for disappearing. They were just happy he was back.

Mom looked at the puppy a bit skeptically and then turned back to Hugo. "And you brought us a new pet to feed . . . ," she said, sounding significantly less thrilled than Zoe. She looked a little concerned.

Hugo whined and playfully nuzzled the puppy with his head.

"It *is* really cute," Sofia said.

"It definitely is!" Dad agreed, getting down on his knees to pet the puppy. Mom took another look at her and smiled.

"You take care of everyone, don't you, Hugo?" she said. "That's why we love you. You must have known this little dog needed a home."

"So we can keep her?" Zoe asked.

"I think we need to take her to the vet and make sure that someone didn't lose her," Mom replied. "But if everything checks out, then I say . . . yes."

"I say yes too," said Dad, smiling.

"Yayyy!" Zoe squealed, clapping her hands and jumping up and down.

"I think this cutie needs a name, doesn't she, Zoe?" Mom asked.

"Um . . . she's brownish gold, and she's *really* sweet," Zoe said, thinking out loud. "Just like waffles! And that's my favorite food! I'm naming her Waffles!"

Waffles barked with delight.

"What do you think of that name?" Hugo asked her.

"It's perfect!" Waffles said, her tail wagging. "Way better than my ideas! It's like the name I always should have had, but never knew! What are waffles? Are they good?"

"I think you'd like them," Hugo replied.

"Come here, boy! Here, Hugo!" Enrique called. He was sitting on the couch in the living room now, away from the family.

Hugo ran over, and Enrique gave him some really phenomenal pets. Then Enrique looked Hugo right in the eyes and spoke softly. "I'm not sure what you got up to today, buddy. But I'm sorry I haven't been paying you enough attention lately. I promise that's going to change. How does this sound? First thing tomorrow, a long walk, just the two of us."

Hugo was thrilled. He wagged his tail and gave Enrique a big fat lick on the face.

"Dinnertime!" Mom called from the kitchen, and Hugo took his usual spot by Sofia's seat, sitting patiently and staring up at the table with his tongue hanging out.

"This is what I do during meals," Hugo explained to Waffles. "You can do it too! It's easy. Just sit wherever you like and stare up at the table!"

"That sounds fun!" Waffles said. "Are you trying to get some of the people food?"

"Nope!" Hugo answered. "Just watching to make sure everyone's having a nice meal."

Waffles nodded, and sat under Zoe's chair.

"But if they *drop* some food on the floor, then I go to town," Hugo added with a smile. "Have you heard of the five-second rule?"

"The five-second rule?" Waffles asked.

"Yeah, if food falls on the floor, I will eat it within five seconds. And it rules."

"Remember, no dessert for you, Enrique!" Mom said. "You're grounded."

Enrique looked sheepishly at the floor.

"I don't know what got into you," Mom said. "Pushing the Roomba down the stairs."

"I've never seen so many pieces," Dad added. "Do you know how long it took me to clean that up?"

"I'm sorry. I don't know what got into me either," Enrique said, shrugging. Then he looked under the table and gave Hugo a little smile. "Maybe I'd just had enough of that Roomba."

Hugo whined happily and put his head on Enrique's lap to say thank you. Enrique nodded and petted his head. So it would be their little secret. Hugo was okay with that.

"How do you clean up the broken pieces of a Roomba?" Dad asked. "You can't use the Roomba!"

Dad laughed at his own joke while the rest of the family rolled their eyes.

"He's funny!" Waffles said to Hugo, wagging her tail. Dad noticed Waffles wagging her tail and rubbed her head.

"Waffles likes my jokes!" Dad said.

"I do! I really do!" Waffles said, but Hugo knew that all the family could hear were happy barks.

Then Hugo had an idea. He motioned for Waffles to follow him across the kitchen. Zoe's backpack was lying on the floor in the corner. He lifted it open with his mouth.

"Wanna go in? It's really fun!" he told her. Waffles wagged her tail and jumped right into the backpack, then turned around so that her head was sticking out the top.

So this is what I looked like back then, Hugo thought. *So funny.*

"Oh my gosh, look!" Sofia called out from the table,

and soon everyone was looking at Waffles and Hugo and cracking up. Enrique started singing, and then the whole family joined in. "Backpack dog! Backpack dog! Waffles is a backpack dog!"

After dinner, the family settled down in the living room to watch the big glowing rectangle together. Enrique picked a nature show. Waffles played on the floor with Zoe, and Hugo sat on the couch with Sofia, resting his head in her lap. He closed his eyes happily.

Today was pretty exciting, Hugo thought. *But there's nothing better than this.*

CHAPTER 13

WHEN LULU ARRIVED at Good Dogs the next morning, Hugo was busy introducing the puppy to all the other dogs.

"Petunia, this is Waffles! Waffles, Petunia!" Hugo said politely.

Petunia stopped wrestling with King for a moment to sniff Waffles up and down. She wagged her tail.

"Nice to meet you, Waffles," Petunia said. "Wrestle later?"

"Sure!" Waffles said enthusiastically as Petunia got back to wrestling with King.

Hugo continued taking Waffles around. "Waffles, meet Cleo. She lives here. Ah, and this is Patches."

"Waffles?" Patches said. "You know, I had a waffle once . . . a long time ago . . . Sit down awhile, I'll tell you all about it."

"So the puppy has a name!" Lulu said as she approached. "I like it."

Lulu noticed that the puppy looked totally different from yesterday. Waffles had clearly had a bath.

"You look so much . . . floofier!" Lulu said. "Kind of like me!"

"Thank you!" Waffles replied as Erin bent over to pet her.

"Always so wonderful to meet a new dog!" Erin said. "We're going to take good care of you here!"

King finished wrestling with Petunia and joined Lulu, Hugo, and Waffles in the front hallway.

"I'm so excited to learn how to be a good dog!" Waffles said to the others. "Just like all of you!"

"Oh, don't get too hung up on being good all the time," Lulu responded, thinking about all of yesterday's adventures. "Sometimes it's nice to just be a dog."

"I second that," Hugo said, nodding knowingly.

"I third it!" King said, holding his head high. Lulu could tell King was excited to be older than someone, and in a position to give advice for once.

"That's why I'm here today, actually," Lulu continued. "To be a dog! Spend some time with ordinary canines, you know. It keeps me humble. Tomorrow I'll be on a movie set with Jasmine. But I like to mix it up."

"That's exciting!" Hugo said. Waffles ran off to

wrestle with Petunia while Lulu brought Hugo and King up to speed.

"Yep! Jasmine got the part!" she said proudly. "*And she wasn't even mad about me getting messy.*"

"That's great! Erin wasn't mad at me either," King replied. "Well, she was worried . . . but she and Cleo were both really happy to see me when I got home."

"Fantastic!" Lulu said. Then she and King turned to Hugo. "How about you?"

"I was so happy to see them," Hugo said. "I thought they wouldn't even notice I was gone, but it turned out they were looking for me the whole time."

Hugo turned to watch as Waffles wrestled happily with Petunia. "And now we have a puppy in the family! They were so happy I came home that they agreed to take her in."

"Wow! Another kid to take care of?" Lulu asked. "That's a lot of extra responsibility! Think you can handle it?"

Hugo smiled as he watched Waffles, and shrugged. "It's what I'm good at," he replied. "When Zoe was born, I wasn't sure I was ready for another kid, but I made it work, and I wouldn't trade it for anything in the world."

Lulu watched Hugo as he watched Waffles play, and she thought that he looked so, so happy. She was sure he'd be a great big brother.

Ding dong! Ding dong! The doorbell rang, and all the dogs naturally started barking with excitement and confusion.

"Who could that be?" Lulu asked.

"I wonder if Erin is expecting mail," King said, wagging his tail and running to the door. "I love mail! And the man who carries the mail! Let's see if I can knock him over!"

Erin held King back as she opened the door, and all the dogs were shocked to see who was on the other side: Napoleon! And one of his people.

Erin seemed surprised too, and she invited Napoleon's mom inside to talk while Napoleon walked over to Lulu, King, and Hugo.

"What are you doing here?" Lulu asked. "Didn't you say that doggy day care was for . . . what did you call us . . . goody two-shoes? Or was it little babies?"

"Oops, I guess I did say that, huh," Napoleon said. "Well, sorry about that. I was just trying to impress you."

"Well, we're excited to see you again," Hugo said.

"My mom thinks something called 'socialization' will be good for me," Napoleon explained. "I don't know what that is, but I hope it tastes good."

They nodded. Lulu was pretty sure "socialization" wasn't a food; she thought it had something to do with Instagram, but she didn't want to correct him.

"Plus, I had fun spending time with you guys yesterday," Napoleon continued. "It's fun being around other dogs. I taught you all how to be bad . . . Maybe I could learn a thing or two about being good?"

"Everybody, listen up!" King announced, jumping onto the couch and barking to get the attention of all the dogs. "This is Napoleon! He's our friend. Napoleon, this is everybody!"

Napoleon wagged his tail as the other dogs barked their greetings. Erin said goodbye to Napoleon's mom and turned her attention to the dogs.

"Time to go to the park!" she said. "Everybody, come sit over here!"

She whistled and Lulu, Hugo, King, and the others walked to the door and sat in a line on her cue. Lulu held her head high, ready for her leash—not because she wanted to be perfect and well behaved, but because she was excited to go to the park and play with her friends. Waffles and Napoleon followed her lead and sat down next to her by the door.

"Am I . . . am I doing this right?" Napoleon asked nervously.

"You're doing great," Lulu whispered back.

"Good boy, Napoleon," Erin said.

Erin leashed them all up, and they started their morning walk through the neighborhood, toward the park. Then through the park and into the dog run. It was the same walk Lulu had done every morning with Erin at Good Dogs, but somehow this morning it felt like everything had changed. Like life was full of new possibilities!

"Everything looks so different now," Hugo said, as if reading her mind.

"And smells different too!" King chimed in.

"It's amazing what one little adventure can do," Lulu said.

Once they got to the dog run, King spotted Nuts running along the top of a bench. "Hey, Nuts!" he called. "Good to see you again."

Nuts smiled and opened his mouth as if to respond, but then his expression changed. "I'm sorry! I just remembered that I'm very, very mad at you!" Nuts huffed and scurried back up into his tree.

"Oh, come on!" Hugo barked up into the tree. "Don't be mad! Dogs love to chase squirrels! It's just something we do! It's nothing personal."

"Really?!" Nuts replied. "So this is just going to be your new thing now, huh? Chasing me?"

Hugo, King, and Lulu looked at one another and shrugged.

Maybe, Lulu thought. She *would* like to do that again. She also barked up into the tree. "You have to admit . . . it was pretty fun."

Nuts just scoffed and turned away, but she could tell he was thinking about it.

"We're all friends here, Nuts," King added. "We were just having fun. But we're sorry if we scared you."

Nuts slowly turned to face them. "Okay. I forgive you," he said. "I have to admit . . . it was *sort of* fun to be chased. Sort of! It had been a while since I'd run like that."

Then he scurried down the tree to get closer to them. He looked like he had something very important to discuss. "Since you're here, I could really use your help," Nuts continued. "I can't seem to find the acorns I buried yesterday."

Lulu, Hugo, and King gave one another a look, as if to say, "This again?"

"They're under the—" Lulu started, but Hugo hastily cut her off.

"Shh! Not so fast," he said to her. Then he turned to Nuts. "We can help you with this problem, if you do something for us in return . . ."

Nuts cocked his head to the side. Lulu understood immediately what Hugo meant, and smiled.

"Let us chase you!" she said. Nuts thought for a moment, then twitched his tail with excitement.

"Okay!" Nuts declared. "That seems like a fair deal."

"You can have a head start," King said. "Ready, set, GO!"

And just like that, Nuts bolted away. He hopped

up onto a bench and ran quickly around the perimeter of the park, hopping from bench to bench and running as fast as he could.

"Hey, Napoleon! Hey, Waffles!" Lulu called as the three of them started to run. "Let's go chase that squirrel!"

Napoleon dropped the stick he was chewing on, and Waffles stopped barking at her shadow. They quickly joined Hugo, Lulu, and King in their high-speed pursuit of the nimble squirrel.

Now they were all running as fast as they could, barking as loud as they could, and having the time of their lives.

ABOUT THE ILLUSTRATOR

TOR FREEMAN (@tormalore) was born in London and received a degree in illustration from Kingston University. She has written and illustrated many children's books and was awarded a Sendak Fellowship in 2012. Tor has also been published in magazines and taught art to students of all ages.

ABOUT THE AUTHORS

RACHEL WENITSKY (@RachelWenitsky) is a comedy writer and actor who has written for *The Tonight Show Starring Jimmy Fallon*, *Saturday Night Live*, and *Reductress*. She is the head writer and a co-host of *The Story Pirates Podcast*, a kids and family podcast on Gimlet Media.

DAVID SIDOROV (@DavidSidorov) is a comedy writer and director who has written for *Alternatino with Arturo Castro*, *Odd Mom Out*, *The Gong Show*, *Billy on the Street*, and *Holey Moley*. He was a field producer and director on *The Rundown with Robin Thede*, and was formerly a writer and director at *The Onion*.

Rachel and David are a married couple living in Brooklyn, New York. This is their first novel. They do not have a dog at the time of writing these bios, but hope that they will by the time you're reading this!

DON'T MISS

GOOD DOGS with BAD HAIRCUTS
Seems like everything goes wrong
when you're having a bad hair day.

And coming soon!

GOOD DOGS in BAD SWEATERS
The holidays can be rough for pups.